Sex Saved The Summer

Momentum never asked permission.
Why should you?

Sex Saved The Summer

Essays and Confessions by

Joseph Adam Lee

Red Fox Runs Press
New York, New York

RED FOX RUNS PRESS
909 3RD AVENUE
#127
NEW YORK, NEW YORK 10150

An imprint of The Rebel Within

First edition: 2026

Publisher's Note

Acknowledgments

Editor: Jennifer Collins
Cover & Layout Design: Eleni Rouketa

Contact Information

Email: joe@therebelwithin.com
Websites: www.josephadamlee.com
Instagram: @joseph.adam.lee

Library Of Congress Cataloging-In-Publication Data

Lee, Joseph Adam. 1986-
Sex Saved the Summer: Essays & Confessions / Joseph Adam Lee.

LCCN: 2025922597

ISBN: 978-1-946673-50-3 (Paperback)
ISBN: 978-1-946673-51-0 (Hardcover)
ISBN: 978-1-946673-53-4 (e-book)
ISBN: 978-1-946673-52-7 (Audiobook)

to *Cameron Stewart*

Author's Note

Names have been changed. Some timelines blurred. In a few places, characters and episodes of my life have been stitched together like bar napkins into a single believable person. This wasn't done to protect anyone's reputation—most of them ruined that on their own—but a little narrative grace was applied where privacy seemed worth keeping.

I painted people the way any writer does: as we need them to fit the story. If a few smudges remain, pardon me. What is a story without embellishment? Perhaps they would have painted themselves differently.

Contents

Sex Saved The Summer

A Royal Rumble on Fire Island

It wasn't a misstep.
It was a public execution.

In New York City, a faux pas can pass as eccentricity—until someone with enough status decides it won't. Few survive such social decay and remain standing. I did.

To understand how I ended up there, you need to understand proximity.

I had just moved to Brooklyn. I was twenty-five. On paper, I looked the part. A polished education. Time at Harvard Medical School. Enough institutional gloss to open doors in a city that mistakes polish for proof. The details held—even though I'd grown up on food stamps, second-hand clothes, and a pride so hard it could make steel quiver.

My initiation into the city's social scene came through the New York Public Library's Young Lions—a posh group camouflaged as intellectual austerity. Less about books, more about being seen around them. Egos held straighter in front of colored spines.

I paid to be a member, which stung—but the perks softened the blow. Membership turned a seven-hundred-dollar gala into something I could afford, along with a year of other NYPL invitations. It was a sanctioned entry into elitist waters.

The night of the gala came. The library lions roared in stone as I passed between them, the city rushing around me like yellow cabs down Fifth Avenue. Inside the ballroom, chandeliers hummed with judgment, champagne flowed, and everyone seemed fluent in a language I was still learning.

I circled the room like a stray dog in a dinner jacket, striking out with small talk and drinking like it was the only language I spoke.

Then, the music caught.

No shuffle. No sway. I danced the way you do when you've got *nothing to prove*. With the kind of improvised moves that pull people in until you're suddenly at the center of the circle.

That's when she noticed me.
Nia.

I noticed her, too. Dark skin, a muted purple gown. She wore a crown—no, just a tiara.

After a round of poppin' and lockin' to early-2000s hip-hop, I drifted toward her.

She meets me halfway—steps loose, deliberate, her rhythm her own. We dance. We pause. We kiss.

I step back. "I'm Joe. Let's get a drink."

Instead, we slip into a dark corner and start making out.

I take a breath. "What do you do?"

Nia coughs. "Who cares? We'll get to that later."

That's when I remember my small act of rebellion—a purple shirt under my tux instead of white. I notice the coincidence in the color of her gown.

"Hey, look at us," I say. "All matching. Like we came here together. Maybe we leave together."

"Mr. Confident," she teases. "You think you own this place?"

"Someone's gotta hold court."

She smiles. "I like you."

I go, "That's what they all say."

Riding the buzz, I step away without breaking eye contact.

"I can't resist," I say, already heading back toward the dance floor.

The gala turns up. Two guys hoist me into the air, my hands raised to the ceiling—then an unceremonious drop back to the floor. Nia's there, pulling me up.

"Let's get out of here. My place," she says.

"Tally-ho!" I slap her ass. She smirks—amused by the boyishness—something she maybe hasn't seen before and, I suspect, won't again.

We rode back to her neighborhood.

In between kisses and sidelong glances, I caught fragments—born in Ghana, raised in Pawling, New York. Movie producer, or something like it.

Then, we arrived. Anywhere, everywhere.

A few things happened once we spilled from the cab—what, exactly, I couldn't tell you. Too much steam. Too much noise in my head to follow the sequence. Faces. Voices. Clinking glasses. Someone saying, "Let's have another one."

Consumption drives us mad. In my case, it drove me straight into a blackout.

When I wake, I'm naked.
I blink into pink. My retinas scorch.
Pink sheets. Pink walls. Pink—everywhere.

I fight the urge to vomit. A breeze sneaks through the window, my palm pressed against the sill. Cold air. A small mercy. Anything to keep my stomach from detonating across the cotton-candy wonderland of her apartment.

To my left, she lies still—slumber, or the imitation of it. Morning-after standoffs go one of two ways: someone speaks, or someone slips out. I'm already planning a clean getaway.

But no. She calls me out. "Good morning. How are you feeling?"

"Feeling great after last night," I lie.

My head burns like shit stewed in gasoline and set on fire.

Then, it hits me. I can't remember her name.

My brain spins, scrambling to cover the amnesia. I steer the conversation toward safer ground—facts, places, anything that might jog memory loose.

"So...fun dance last night. Where did we go after? What was that place called?"

Bits of the slideshow flicker back. A cab ride. A stranger getting out at his stop—then pausing, clocking our gala attire, and slipping the cab driver a twenty.

"You kids have some fun tonight," he said. "This one's on me."

Then, blurrier—a dive bar we had no business in. It smelled like the belly of a ship. Faces rough. Teeth optional.

"Oh—Barley's. Down by Washington Square," she says. "It was nice to get a drink there."

"How did we get back here?" I ask—meaning her place.

She laughs, pointing out the window. "Joe, Barley's is right around the corner."

The pieces returned. Her name didn't.

I was sure it started with an N.
Neema. Naphka.
Wrong. Both of them.

"I've got to run to the ladies' room," she says with a wink.

The moment the door closes, I burst into investigation—desperate to know who the hell I've slept with, and why everything is so damn pink. I scan the studio apartment. Sorority relics everywhere—Kappa Kappa Gamma paddles, framed photos, a shrine to college glory. No diploma bearing a name. But a Yale sweater folded neatly on the dresser.

Next stop: the desk. Mail. Thank God for the United States Postal Service.

Nia Brooks.

At least I hadn't fucked a ghost.

She emerges. "Everything okay, hun?"

Hun? Red flag. I play along anyway.

"Yeah, babe—everything's great." I search for my things. "Really gotta get to work...trying to find my—"

"Your clothes are on that chair by the door," she says, sweet as sugar, something sharp underneath.

"Oh—yeah. Of course." I grab my pants, fumble with my zipper. "Great night. We should do it again."

"Sure," she says. "My number, right?"

I nod.

She takes my phone. "I'll put it in for you. You remember my name, right?"

One hand on her hip—married-ten-years energy.

"Of course," I say. "Nia." I bow, mock-ceremonial majesty.

The dash to work is one of the worst—and best—moments of my life. Best, because I finally feel like I'm living a true New York existence: gala, afterparty, one-night stand, moral hangover—and the faint chance that I need penicillin.

Alcohol still crawled through my veins as I slipped into the office building in a full tuxedo—collar limp, bow tie dangling—more costume than suit now. I waved at the security guard and felt it. A throb in my shoulder. A souvenir from the dance floor.

By the time I hit my desk, the disguise came off. I pulled on my teal scrubs—the only uniform in the city that lets you pass from champagne to coffee without explanation.

My first order of business wasn't medical research. I had more personal investigation to do.

Google. Instagram. LinkedIn. The holy trinity of curated identity.

Nia Brooks... Click.

First: royal lineage. Ashanti. Ghana. A princess. From Africa.

Second: the résumé. Pawling childhood. Yale undergrad. Now—NYU film school. Credits include *A Furious Sound* (producer). Awarded the Silver Prize by the New York Independent Film Society. One reviewer gushed, *"A force to be reckoned with—gets the job done under budget. Tough cookie. Expect big things."*

So far, so good—until I saw what came up next.

Years earlier, I'd trained myself to tack *scam* onto any name before committing to jobs, purchases, or vacations. I figured it could save me from bad dates, too.

Sure enough, Reddit was waiting.

I typed: *Nia Brooks + scam.*

Skeletons in the closet. The commentary read:

"Scam artist. Crook. Don't trust this BITCH."

"Deceiver. Diva. Pockets per diem money."

It read like an HR director's private meltdown. I felt the hesitation creep back in.

Then, at 1 p.m., a text lit up my phone: *Hey, hun. Hope work's okay. Hang soon?*

I thought about it. Résumé versus Reddit. Crown versus con.

I decided to ignore the text. Not out of strategy, but instinct. Something didn't add up.

Months passed. No contact. I moved on.

Then, out of nowhere, another text: *Come over tonight?*

A booty call.

Another man might've gone for it, but I didn't. Not emotionally—and, if I'm honest, not financially either. Cab fare. Condoms. Breakfast. It all added up to thirty or forty bucks—money better spent on beer, pizza, and laundry.

I texted: *Not feeling up to it.*

She replied with a flat: *Night.*

And that was that—or so I thought. But New York doesn't do clean exits. It recycles its characters and drags them back onstage whether you're ready or not.

The island runs on recurrence.

Meanwhile, I was putting down roots. Appearance was enough—at least at first. Reputation lagged behind presence. Your referral was whoever stood next to you.

That's how I met Pat.

I was living with a couple of NYU grads—rotating roommates, rotating guests. One of them invited Pat over one night. Pat showed up with two friends: Jerry and Mickey.

I remember Pat less for his face than for his outfit: a green velvet blazer, bright blue pants, and boat shoes. It was 2011—a hinge year in fashion, when J.Crew and Ralph Lauren started partying with Salvatore Ferragamo. Reclaimed preppy was drifting from Nantucket toward Lake Como. Hence the velvet blazer at a Brooklyn house party, in a neighborhood where most people couldn't afford bread, let alone a knife to slice it.

"That's a great jacket," I said. Earnest. No irony.

Pat looked at me, surprised. Most people didn't compliment things like that out loud anymore.

"I had a pink one," I added. "Ralph Lauren. Wore it until it fell apart."

He smiled—the kind that says you've passed a small but important test.

From there, the night loosened. Drinks appeared. Introductions followed.

Jerry was taller and sharper. The type who wore thrifted leather jackets like rent was a myth. His side hustle was older, wealthy women—as if that counted as a profession.

Mickey lingered at the edges, quiet, but his eyes did most of the work—half-smiling like the joke was unfolding three steps ahead of you.

Pat was the son of a movie producer. He always had a plan.

By the end of the night, I was folded into their inner circle.

With Pat's pull, I leaned into the city. Fully immersed in the twenty-something lifestyle—bars, boats, brunches. We cross-pollinated friend groups like amateur social engineers.

But as much as I wanted to avoid it, there was a hierarchy at work. One built on access. Friendship wasn't just companionship; it was contribution.

I moved quickly, earning my keep.

I dug up a cheap "benefit" with an open bar—a fifty-dollar harbor cruise for leukemia or some such cause—and bought tickets for the group. "I've got this one," I said.

Mickey earned his place differently—dinners at one of his father's restaurants, on the house, endless wine, and the kind of bill no one ever saw.

Jerry had immunity. He didn't need to earn anything. He and Pat went back to grade school. History outranked contribution. Every time.

But every win expired fast, replaced by a new test, a fresh expectation. Every night out ended the same way—with the same unspoken questions: *What's next? Can you keep up?*

That's where I had to tap out every so often. When plans called for five-hundred-a-head bottle service, I bowed out. I'd find myself in conversations like:

"I've got work early tomorrow."

"On a Sunday?" they'd ask.

"Yeah—even on a Sunday."

The truth wasn't workplace allegiance. I wanted to party, but I could hardly afford pasta, let alone Grey Goose with Sarah Lawrence girls who'd known Pat since prep school.

That was the burden I carried—trying to convince the room I was enough. No one suspected otherwise but me. Still, I lasted long enough to get an invite to Pat's family's house.

Which is how we ended up on Fire Island.

Fire Island wasn't Coney Island. It wasn't Rockaway. It was private, seasonal, curated—a place where people went to be seen only by the right people. A weekend away revealed more than any random night out ever could. Excursions showed how you carried yourself outside the city... how you handled the chaos of ferries, the sting of thirty-dollar lobster rolls, and the locals' sideways looks.

Pat spelled out one stipulation—half-joking, but I took it seriously: "Everyone, bring a girl."

I needed more than just any girl. I needed someone who could tilt the room—someone who'd walk into that beach house and make the others think: *She belongs here.*

So, I thought of Nia.

I had reservations. Aside from our romantic hiatus, even if she agreed to go, I worried about how I'd read next to Pat. Would she see me as anything more than a stepping stone?

Maybe I was overthinking it.

So, I broke code. No text. I called her.

"Do you want to go to Fire Island for the weekend?" I asked. It was only a week away.

Nia answered fast, disbelief in her voice. "For real? I want to go, but are you actually inviting me?"

"Should be fun," I said. "We'd stay at my friend's place. Two nights."

"Sleep over? Yes!" She paused. "Well...I hurt my leg. It's in a boot. Is that okay?"

I pictured a Bond-girl beach entrance gone wrong—the camera gliding from her face to her curves, then stopping cold at a Velcro-strapped orthopedic boot.

Still, the pressure was on, so I joked, "You and boot are both welcome."

A week later, I climbed the stairwell to her place, the steps rising like an archway to a crown. Between knocks, I heard her hobbling toward the door. *Swing, plant, hobble*—like a Lincoln Log missing a joint. The door opened to yet another surprise. To complete the pirate look, she wore an eye patch, recovering from a nasty sty.

"Arrr, matey," I couldn't help myself. "Ready for the voyage?"

She waved it off, unamused.

Fortunately, she ditched the patch before we met the guys who were waiting in a rented SUV. Pat's doing, of course. To my surprise, none of them had a girl with them. To their astonishment, I'd pulled through.

Mickey leaned in. "Dude. Nice score."

"I thought everyone was bringing someone?" I asked.

He shrugged. "We failed. I'll meet someone on the island anyway."

That's when the resentment crept in. I sat there, squeezed into the middle seat between Nia and Mickey, feeling it settle in. Nia knew exactly how to play it. She grabbed my hand and nuzzled into me like we'd been dating for months.

By the time we hit the highway, she launched right in.

"Joe and I met a while ago. The timing was off, but I always thought about him. When he asked me to be his date for this weekend, I was elated. How could I say no? I think lil Joey and I are ready to rekindle some flames."

"Lil Joey?" Mickey nudged me.

My eyes rolled so hard, I felt it in my spine.

After forty minutes, we parked at the ferry depot. I grabbed Nia and my bag and headed for the boat, humiliation doing the walking for me.

Thirty minutes later, we were on Fire Island.

I learned fast that the island is carved into territories—each with its own vibe, its own tribe. Most people imagine it as a nonstop party haven for the gay community—and that's part of it—but there are also pockets where old money meets newcomers, gay meets straight, and locals meet weekenders, all blending under the same sun.

Our territory was in Ocean Beach.

My expectations were low, but Pat outdid himself. Bikes were waiting for us, each with a trolley hitched behind it for our bags.

"No car?" I asked.

Pat laughed. "No cars. Just bikes. Paths everywhere—you cruise, you wave. That's it."

He wasn't kidding. Bikes were everywhere. Unlocked. Leaning against railings, waiting for their next rider. The place felt safe, communal—the kind of setup that only works if everyone agrees to play along.

Even Nia had her own set of wheels, pedaling surprisingly well despite the boot. Watching her glide, I couldn't help but wonder how much of that limp I'd imagined.

We arrived at Pat's family beach house—huge, right on the sand. Everything you'd expect and more. Lucky little beach rats, we were. Even Nia shot me a look of approval, as if I'd personally booked the place.

Sometimes, life works out that way.

We started sorting out sleeping arrangements when Pat said, "I had you with Mickey, but since you're with Nia, you can take the private room. I'll bunk with him."

The word *with* lodged in me like a splinter.

"Thanks, Pat."

I lugged her Louis Vuitton bags upstairs. She followed, slower. I'd barely set the bags down before she pulled me in, kissed me hard, unapologetic, and whispered, "Fuck me. Now."

I obeyed.

As the foreplay picked up, she suddenly barked—more drill sergeant than seductress—"Suck those titties like there's milk in them."

My brain immediately flagged the request as biologically implausible. Then, it moved on to the math—erotic geometry complicated by a dead-leg boot.

I went for it anyway.

Afterwards, I felt strangely untethered.

"Hey," I said. "What's the arrangement here?"

She smirked. "Oh dear, no. This is purely an F-and-F Weekend."

"A...what?"

"Fun-and-Fuck Weekend. No strings attached."

"Okay," I said slowly. "What if I meet someone tonight?"

"That's fine," she said. "Same goes for me. But if we feel like a quickie in between—" She hooted, flashing a peace sign. "Why the hell not? It's an F-and-F Weekend!"

Still, I wasn't blind to the problem. Sharing a room. Already entangled. *So be it*, I thought.

We geared up for the first night out—bar-hopping between Albatross, CJ's, and Hideaway. Pat knew all the spots and all the faces. Introductions rolled out like résumés on speed. Sprints of inconsequential status factoids sounded:

"We used to ski together in Switzerland."

"Our families went to Bermuda once."

Fifteen-second pitches of credibility. Gone the second you walked away.

The final stop was Matthew's Seafood House, the island's late-night anchor. Packed wall to wall. Neon lights turning every white shirt radioactive purple. Tropical drinks—ninety percent booze, ten percent mystery dye. No AC—just ceiling fans pushing the heat around like a lazy dealer shuffling cards.

Pat knew the owners, so we got the VIP treatment—our own table, bottle service, the manager shouting over the music, "Tell your dad I said hi!" while "Mr. Brightside" blasted from the DJ booth.

With a chilled bottle of Grey Goose on display, attention came easy. People came to us.

When I started talking to another girl, Nia slid in effortlessly—charming, generous, redirecting the focus until the moment turned back to her again. It wasn't territorial, exactly. Just precise. And it left me oddly disoriented.

The night blurred us back to the house.

I slid into bed beside Nia.
Nothing more. Nothing less.
No romance. No fights.

I stumbled into the kitchen the following morning, head pounding.

"Where's Mickey?" Pat asked.

"Your guess is as good as mine," I said.

Pat's phone buzzed. He glanced down.

"Oh, he's at the police station," Pat replied, like he was telling me the weather.

"Huh?"

"Fred just texted me."

"Fred?"

"Went to high school with him. He's a cop here now—family lives two doors down."

No surprise on Fire Island. An endless loop of familiar faces. Everyone either grew up together or was sleeping with someone who did.

"Joe, come ride with me. We'll pick him up, then grab supplies for tonight."

"Supplies?"

"Yeah. We're hosting a party at the house. Food, booze, all that. My brother's coming, too—he'll probably be at the ferry dock by the time we're done."

We left the house and biked over to the police station. Mickey was sprawled outside on a bench, still drunk.

"What a night, huh?!" He grinned. "I was on the beach with that sweet baby—making out, going down on her. Let's do it again tonight!"

I'll admit—I was jealous. But also weirdly proud.

"Sounds great," Pat said flatly. "Let's hit the market before the noon rush."

I was struck by how unbothered he was—as if picking up your drunk friend from the police station was just another square on the Fire Island weekend bingo card. Then again, we needed to beat the locals to the store before the steaks and watermelon disappeared.

At the market, we loaded up. Not just snacks, but full spreads: chicken cutlets, veggie skewers, tropical fruit, coconut shavings for dessert. Pat waved off our offers to chip in.

"You're guests," he said.

That was Pat's understated class—hosting without ever making it feel like hosting.

We met his brother Mel at the ferry—the same face as Pat's, only bulkier from college rugby. All shoulders, no neck. The four of us biked back to the house, stashed the haul, and headed straight for the beach.

Nia wore a 1950s-style bikini with enough fabric to double as a picnic blanket—and, of course, the plastic-wrapped boot. She parked herself next to Jerry, the two of them locked in conversation like background characters who'd found each other. Apparently, they bonded over conspiracy documentaries—chemtrails, JFK, even the Loch Ness monster.

I was grateful. It gave me a breather from Nia's not-but-kind-of boyfriend duty.

Pat and I walked the shoreline. "What's the real deal with her?" he asked.

"Nothing serious," I said.

He nodded, then added—polite, precise—"She kind of works in the group."

I watched Nia laughing with Jerry, fitting neatly into our crew, and understood what Pat meant. Here, chemistry mattered less than calibration—whether someone could occupy space without tipping it. Nia knew this and made it look easy.

Everything held that afternoon, with that lazy summer illusion that youth, beauty, and access might last forever. But they never do. We found out why later that night.

Pat's house was packed—same chatter as the night before, just louder, sweatier, with bodies layered into every corner. Music bled through the walls. People shouted to be heard. The air felt damp with alcohol and sunscreen.

I ducked into the bathroom to regroup. That's where I found Nia—pressed against the sink, lips locked with some guy. The door hadn't even been closed.

She pulled back the second she saw me. Her eyes widened—not guilt exactly, more panic.

"It's not what you think," she said quickly. "It just happened."

To her surprise, I wasn't angry. I felt light. Relieved, even.

"Hey," I said quietly. "You said it yourself—Fun-and-Fuck Weekend."

She stared at me, waiting for something else—jealousy, control, a scene. When none came, her expression shifted. Confusion first. Then something sharper.

Outside, the guys caught my eye across the room.

"You good?" Pat asked.

"Totally fine," I said, shrugging. "I'll find someone new tonight."

It wasn't a declaration. It was logistics.

Hours later, at Matthew's Seafood House, Nia and her new guy were glued together. I'd like to say it didn't bother me, but booze has a way of turning jealousy into strategy. So, I found a gorgeous brunette named Carol, and within minutes, we were kissing.

I flashed the guys a thumbs-up—until Carol's hair snapped back in a hard yank.

Nia. *Screeching.*

"Enough already! This is my boyfrieeeennnd, by the way!"

And just like that—a royal rumble on Fire Island.

It wasn't a couple's fight, but it looked like one. The kind that needs witnesses so it can later be dismissed as something we just had to get out of our system.

I was furious. Nia, I assume, was hurt. Desire doesn't negotiate.

We spilled into the street—me held back by Pat and Mickey, Jerry gripping Nia. Lines drawn. Sides picked. Then, the police rolled up.

Pat called out, "Hey, Fred—sorry! Night two of my friends stirring up trouble."

Fred grinned. "Wouldn't be Fire Island, otherwise."

Jerry led Nia away, spellbound—the kind of devotion only the wounded inspire.

I stayed behind, less heartbroken than worried. My real fear wasn't her—it was whether the guys now saw me as the liability. I'd worked too hard to get inside this circle.

The last thing I wanted was to be the guy who burned it down.

That night, I slept far from her. Pat and Mel offered me their old room—a bunk bed, Mel on top and me on the bottom. I passed out the second my head hit the pillow. No dreams. No tossing. Just the dead sleep of someone who'd had enough drama for one weekend.

When I woke, my eyes begged for moisture.
My contacts had dried into my corneas.
Like I'd fallen asleep with retainers in my eyes.

By then, it was already past noon. We shuffled out to start the day. No one mentioned the fight, but we all wore it in our posture.

"You guys hungry?" Pat asked.

We all conceded.

He suggested lunch at a Japanese place. We sat cross-legged at low tables, the air thick with soy sauce and grilled fish. A few rounds of sake later, the tension softened. I kept things light, poked fun at myself, and made sure no one felt iced out.

That's when I noticed Nia's eyes relaxing, her mouth easing toward a smile.

"How can I stay mad at you?" she asked, almost to herself.

It struck me—again—that conflict can sharpen attraction.
Not because pain is pleasurable, but because friction leaves evidence.

By the time we rode back toward the ferry, the whole weekend felt almost staged—like the fight had been a scene, and now we were in the aftermath, where everyone pretends they remember their lines.

We docked and drove back to the city.

Pat dropped Nia and me at her place. Even in my scorn, I volunteered to carry her bags up the steps. She thanked me, that familiar knowing smile returning as if nothing had ever happened.

I turned to leave. One hand on the door.

She stopped me. "Hey—wait."

"Yes?"

She twinkled.

"Joe, we're going to date and see how it goes."

"What?" I waited just long enough to keep composure. "I don't think that's a good idea. This weekend was enough." I pitched it gently, as if sparing her from making a mistake.

The words ricocheted. She stood there absorbing them—as if already planning her next move, with the patience of someone who plays chess against those who only know checkers.

"No," she said finally. "This weekend was silliness. We're starting to understand each other. Let's see where this goes."

I knew this didn't feel right. Was almost dangerous.
But whatever this was between us already had a grip.

I saw the certainty in her—the assumption that things would bend her way. That there would be room for me if I wanted to stay in the game.

If I walked away, I might not get another shot.

So, I agreed to see her again.

What happened next didn't just shift the relationship. It escalated it.

11:26 a.m. on Tuesday, I got a text: *Can you meet tonight for an invite-only early screening?*

I asked which movie.

The Wolf of Wall Street.

For a certain kind of up-and-coming New Yorker, the movie is the ultimate fantasy—edge, ego, excess. Leonardo DiCaprio's Jordan Belfort ascends through pure appetite: booze, blow, broads. A three-hour carnival of indulgence disguised as cinema.

At first, I didn't believe the invite was real. I half-expected a bait-and-switch—some obscure bar, the screening mysteriously "canceled," the night rerouted back to Nia's apartment and its familiar gravity.

Then, she pulled through. Nia sent the details.

6:30 p.m. arrival.
Undisclosed Venue.
Screening at 7:00 sharp.

I'm technically still sworn to secrecy about where it was held, but let's just say it wasn't your average AMC. My phone was taken at the door—no pockets, no excuses. From there, I was led downward into what felt like a secret passage, one of those movie staircases hidden behind a bookshelf. The kind lit by wax-dripped candelabras that somehow never burn the hand holding them.

At the base, a giant golden statue loomed.

An Oscar.

I asked, "Why is that here?"

She smirked. "This is the Academy's theater."

I blinked.

"Early screening," she added. "Producers. Academy voters."

The room ripened instantly. But it didn't stop there.

I nudged her, pointing toward a familiar profile. "Is that Martin Scorsese?"

She nodded. "Yeah. Over there's Margot Robbie. Next to her—DiCaprio."

I sat there, dumbfounded.

And yes—since you're wondering—I met them all.

When I finally rubbed shoulders with Leonardo DiCaprio, he was as dreamy as ever. I didn't let the awe stop me from congratulating him on his performance. Smooth, maybe. Shaky, definitely. But I meant it.

Nia had already cornered Margot Robbie, speaking toward some obscure fact she knew about Robbie's hometown in Queensland—maybe a beach where she'd shot an early ad campaign, or a pub her uncle once owned. Small talk delivered with a precision that made it feel suddenly essential. I was introduced briefly. Margot Robbie kissed me on the cheek.

Of course, it was nothing. Still, I couldn't resist the feeling. As if the peck were a pardon—an early entry through heaven's gate.

By the time we left, word had already leaked about Leo's whereabouts. Someone had tipped off the paparazzi. My guess: a burner phone smuggled into the theater, followed by a flurry of texts to hungry photographers.

As he prepared to exit, DiCaprio turned to me and said, "Mind walking me to my car?"

No handholding—though if he'd asked, I would have. It was, after all, Leonardo DiCaprio.

Sunglasses on. Hat dipped. He leaned into me like we were old friends, and I parted the crowd like a decoy. Just before stepping into the car, he looked back and said, "Thanks for making a path, man."

I went back inside, still dazed from the paparazzi bulbs that had washed my vision away.

Nia met me at the coat check, beaming. She knew exactly what she had done.

"Told you I'd be worth dating," she said. "Plenty of perks."

I'll admit I was seduced by the arrangement—the tacit agreement that let me move through velvet ropes unscathed. Who'd have thought the son of a welder from Lewiston, Maine would end up inside a palace built of press passes, perfume, and borrowed bravado?

It wasn't a dream.
It was worse.
It was real.

And, for a while, I belonged.

During my run with Nia and the boys, the gang drifted deeper into excess. We were the city's indulged kids, playing dress-up as adults—riding the tear-streaked fantasy: young, free, and all parts brat.

Eventually, the seams showed. Fantasies come with an expiration date. Mine just happened to be stitched in cursive on a monogrammed napkin I couldn't afford to stain.

By then, Nia and I had been circling each other for three months—long enough for patterns to form, short enough to pretend they didn't mean anything yet. Somewhere in those strange, seductive circumstances, something darker was taking shape.

Our last night revealed it.

It started with a magazine event—*Robb Report*. One of those high-gloss lifestyle spreads celebrating private jets and curated cigars, where even the waitstaff look like they have agents. I'd wrangled an invite. Naturally, Nia was my plus-one.

Everything was bespoke. Ice cut into spheres. Cocktails with backstories.

The afterparty spilled onto the rooftop of the James Hotel, where Pat and the boys were already waiting. We sat high above the city, wrapped in the skyline.

For a moment, it felt like I'd made it.

Then came Eftalya.

Nia had invited her to join us—she was a smoke show from Turkey, some hybrid of fashion publicist and beauty brand founder. She claimed her new serum could "retrain your skin's memory." One jar of papaya and ancestral lipids ran two hundred dollars, packaged like it had been smuggled out of the Grand Bazaar.

I wouldn't call what happened flirting—but Nia did. Apparently, I was making a move on her friend.

"Joe, you're trouble," Eftalya said, grazing my shoulder.

Nia saw it. Minutes later, the two of them disappeared into the bathroom.

When they returned, Eftalya was a shade colder.

Nia pulled me aside and said, "Leave Eftalya alone."

"Stop acting like you own me," I said.

"I've always owned you!" she shot back—loud enough for the group to hear.

So, I threatened to leave. "You know what? I'm out."

"Good. Leave." Nia scowled.

She paused, then aimed.

"You've always just been some poor white trash from Maine anyhow."

She caught me off guard. Everyone else, too. This wasn't our usual Nia-and-Joe tit-for-tat. This was lower. *Meaner*. A swing meant to end the fight, not win it.

I should have let it slide. But in that moment—ignore or ignite—I couldn't keep the match unlit. Booze fanned a shame years in the making.

I struck back with the worst defense imaginable. A trembling confession.

"I just got a raise today. I can pay for anything now."

In that room, it sounded like begging.

No amount of sway—not even from Pat—was going to change it. Moments like this reveal proximity's limits. When hierarchy reveals itself, even the kind ones go still.

Their place was secure.
Mine never had been.

I was no longer a name among the stars. Just another body below the line.

I never saw the guys again after that night. No confrontation. No goodbye. Just distance, doing what distance does best.

I crossed paths with Nia a few times afterward. An event here or there. We didn't speak. I'd nod. I'd kiss the ring—not out of love, but fear of falling out of view.

One last time—an early screening of the film adaptation of Jack Kerouac's *On the Road*.

Afterwards, I decided to approach her.

"Long time no see," I said.

She looked straight past me. "Sorry, I don't think I know you."

She wasn't wrong. She didn't know me.

I was a yellow Roman candle.

Burn.
Burn.
Burn.

The Opulent Squatter

The morning was brutal.
The day ahead promised worse.

As if the looming worry of whether Benjamin—our apartment squatter—would be gone by evening wasn't enough, the lingering aroma of weed and Marlboros made sure I suffered. The wound was salted by last night's filth—a countertop congregation of every hipster's party pal—Stella, Amstel, Coors, Modelo, Pabst—the empties lined up like sponsors of my slow demise.

I tiptoed around island-shaped films of dried hops toward the bathroom.

Inside, the porcelain quarters glistened in yard-sale proportions. Leftover cocaine calcified in neon-green, blue, and pink inch-square packets—all scattered across the floor like plastic Easter eggs waiting to be cracked open. I thought about taking a bump, but I resisted.

The dubstep rattled the walls. My roommate Jake, the self-proclaimed DJ Jake the Snake (named after his childhood wrestling hero), had the sound system cranked, blasting MGMT at peak decibel: *"Shock me like an electric eel."*

My uneven brain swayed. I flushed.
Molasses-colored ghosts spiraled out of sight.

Even my piss had become cliché.

I meandered upstairs, climbing the stairwell from the basement of our five-bedroom duplex like a pilgrim nursing a cornucopia-sized hangover. Settlers littered the path—on couches, on floors, maybe even out on the sidewalks. Who the hell knew what they'd discovered about themselves last night? All these human bodies, passed out in angles, ready for pick-up in body bags—each one a soft blockade between me and my holy trinity: eggs, toast, and yes, always, orange juice.

I drank straight from the carton. All the cups were either missing or fermenting in a sink full of dishwater and regret. Fruit flies hovered like helicopter paparazzi. I swatted one and sent it into a see-sawing death spiral until it landed, raisin-like, on the cheek of Benjamin, who always seemed to pass out in the kitchen, like a pauper warmed by the mercy of a working stove.

With two eggs scrambling and the juice already in my stomach, I reached for the toast—crisp and golden, maybe too perfect for a morning like this. But the stench, the gin flashbacks, the faint smell of drywall and desperation...I forced the urge to retch back down. I covered my plate with a paper towel, slid it into the fridge, and hoped my craving would return before the mold.

Just as I closed the fridge door, a hand reached past me.

"Hey, you gonna eat that?" Benjamin asked, eyes reeling with anticipation.

"Yeah, man. Fuck off. Go back to sleep," I said, sealing the door shut.

Even a comfy beggar asks for more.

But to understand how we'd gotten stuck with him, I need to rewind six months—to where the mess actually began.

It was 2015 in Crown Heights, Brooklyn. My first New York City apartment.

Five of us lived together—Jake, Jorge, Mike, Isaac, and me. A chance union born from one Craigslist post and an overeager desire to forge friendship through a sublease. Every one of us was young, beautiful, and restless, though redundancy flowed through us like a shared bloodstream. The weekly routine recycled itself like half-chewed gum passed from mouth to mouth.

Weekend 1: "Let's go to the brick-oven pizza joint. Get dinner and drinks."
All: "Yeah, good idea."

Weekend 2: "Brick-oven pizza joint? I still can't believe what you did there last week, Jake."
All: "Yeah, good idea."

Eventually, even the crust tasted like déjà vu.

Sparks of change would flare up, but most died with the fire of a cigarette butt. Yet, even among the strings of ashes, something citrus lingered—bitter, sweet, elusive. The urge to create was a constant topic of conversation. Loud in banter, tepid in execution.

"I'm going to write a screenplay."
Two months later: "How's that screenplay?"
"I'm still trying to find my inspiration. It has to be just right, you know?"

It all became a buffer against reality. The egotism of it was ironic. Everyone was obsessed with themselves, yet no one stood alone. Each person simultaneously relied on themselves *and* on everyone else...for validation, for attention, for proof they mattered.

In truth, the group *itself* was the egotist.

But the strangest part wasn't the intoxication, or the faux brilliance everyone floated on like helium, or the dull ache of watching all that flaunting finally pop. It was something else—it was boarding strangers who became friends who became squatters.

A squatter is someone who occupies a space without paying rent. Simple enough. I was used to friends crashing for the weekend—but baked into those visits is an unspoken agreement: *This is my place. You are a guest. You will leave soon.*

That's exactly how we treated Benjamin at first—as another guest passing through. But he lingered. And lingered.

One house party was all it took.

Benjamin was older than all of us—a thirty-something Brit dropped into a pack of New Englanders still smelling of undergrad. I swear he was built out of angles—like an amateur sketch of the Tin Man on one of those red Etch A Sketches. Never round, never fluid. Just sharp movements, junkyard-bent, like scrap metal given legs.

His clothes draped off him in tired sheets, and when he walked, his limbs swung with an eerie, underwater grace. The first time I met him, one of his tentacles found me while I was grabbing a beer from the fridge. I remember feeling his arm, his chest, his ribs—bones barely disguised by a thin sheath of acrylic fabric.

He drew closer.

As if no one else existed, he said in a raspy English accent, "You're a nose breather."

Then, going from his navel to his furrowed brow, his other tentacle moved methodically—like a maestro conducting a breathing exercise.

He traced the motion upward from the diaphragm and released it down through the nostrils.

A nose breather.

Hmm. Peculiar. But it beat the standard exchange of small-talk pleasantries.

Benjamin, in a sense—and with full pun intended—was a breath of fresh air. Looking back, I'd say my roommates and I needed a Benjamin to break through our daily doldrums. If anything, we saw him as an abnormality. That excited us. And, to this day, I think it's always been the misfits who remind us that being normal isn't freedom. No, it's the sign you've already traded freedom away.

Benjamin continued with his tantric nose philosophy.

"Well, mate—there are two types of people out there. Those that breathe through their noses, and those other dink types—the sloth mouth breathers..."

Then, he leaned in, pitching his voice lower now, as if whispering a secret between two old souls.

"Mouth breathers are the pigs on Wall Street. Cookie cutters. Basically anti-art protestors."

He paused, his face puckering as if he'd just bitten into a chunk of piercing, bluish-green cheese.

"Grooooossssss."

He made a spitting motion, like the offense still lingered on his tongue, then shifted his wrinkled gaze back toward me. His ashtray breath seemed to smoke on its own. I caught the outline of his face—narrow goatee, greased ponytail—before he continued.

"I always try to surround myself with nose breathers. They're pure. Better thinkers. They actually take time to observe...you know."

He waited. Watched me. Searched my face. I had nothing.

"Mouth breathers..." He moved closer, his lips now perspiring on my earlobe. "...are rubbish in bed."

A beat.

He gave me a sensual look. "They don't know how to breathe when they're, you know..." His fingers drifted downward, tracing my breastbone. "...down there."

He tapped my crotch.
Gently—like checking a melon for ripeness.

I laughed.
The ice finally broke.

Benjamin grabbed me by the neck like he was roping a calf, kissed my forehead, and slurred, "Fah-uckin'...love this pissah."

His charisma had caught me.
Soon enough, it caught my roommates, too.

As our household became the epicenter of weekend debauchery, we found endless chances to display our mutual fascination. Benjamin became the lubricant for our dried-out delusions, letting us play poets while we drifted in circles with white powder, starless nights, and the kind of permission only youth ever grants.

But Benjamin didn't limit himself to the weekends; his presence came with no hiatus at all.

Fortunately for him, Jake invited him over often. They had a natural bond—instantaneous, and faster than you'd expect from two men not in love. It wasn't romantic. It was philosophical.

They'd sit in the living room for hours reading the same news articles, debating like auditors of a political science professorship they were convinced was already theirs.

"Socialism is on the brink in America, mate—look at this editorial the *Times* wrote about Barack," Benjamin would say, holding up the paper like it had earned him an A+.

Jake would nod gravely, eyes sharp. "Trump is pure capitalism," he countered. "His rise is already tyrannical."

Benjamin smirked. "You think he could really be President next year?"

Jake shrugged, almost reverently. "In this country? Whoever pays to play wins."

Benjamin leaned back, pleased with himself. "2016 is going to be a year full of flames."

Jake cracked a thin smile. "Burnt by the buck."

The two of them would then snarl at each other—not with contempt, but with something eerily close to seduction. Lines were never crossed, but the chemistry was undeniable.

Soon, Benjamin wasn't just around—he was unavoidable.

It all came to a pulp when Jake called an apartment meeting on the last Thursday of September. The conversations started with a vague text: *Hey guys, can we meet later? It's about Benjamin. He needs our help.*

I hated that message. Text leaves too much room for disaster.

I fired back: *What's happening?*

No reply.

By 5 p.m., when I got home, the others were already in the living room—Jorge, Mike, and Isaac—each wearing the same anticipatory wrinkle between their brows. The front door opened right into it.

Jake was in the kitchen, making a sandwich. "Oh hey, man."

"Yep. So, what's up?" I asked.

He cleared his throat and drifted toward the living room. I followed, already braced.

"Well...the Benjamin situation. His lease is up at the end of the week."

We knew what came next.

"Do you think he can crash here for a bit? Everyone cool with that?"

The question was rhetorical.

Not only had Jake been galvanized by Benjamin, he was also the sole leaseholder—and, implicitly, the one who decided who stayed and, more importantly, who had to pay rent.

The rest of us weren't bothered. Maybe we were naïve, maybe just riding the wave, but we didn't see the harm. We liked Benjamin, then. A silent shrug rippled through the room, eye to eye.

Agreement established.

We figured he'd be there for a few weeks, maybe a month. Just long enough for him to land on his feet.

To his credit, he played the guest role beautifully. At least for the first few days.

Benjamin cleaned daily, walked Hero—our rescue mutt—and even made a surprisingly solid macaroni and cheese with sausage. A dish he somehow converted us onto.

Benjamin even cleaned the bathroom once—whistling the Sex Pistols and spraying lavender Lysol like a Mary Poppins with a nicotine addiction.

But a few weeks stretched into a month, and the charm wore thin.

Then came the smells.

Dirty clothes. Yellow pit stains. No problem—he'd just cut off the sleeves. The odor? A full-blown bacterial insurrection. Gross? Yeah, it was.

Eventually, Isaac and I grabbed his cardboard box of clothes and hauled it to the laundromat. We felt like criminals the entire time—soap-and-suds thieves on the run. Would our goodwill register as an insult? As if cleaning his clothes violated his independence, and *we* were the ones who should apologize?

We were wrong to worry. He never noticed.

You ever have someone use your razor? Gross, but forgivable—a kind of masculine communion. Still, I'd wince when the occasional nick left the blade crusted red. I told myself that warm water rinses away blood-borne pathogens.

Doesn't it?

The line was drawn when he used my toothbrush. Benjamin had this tar-dark stain above his top teeth—dentists probably have a name for it, but I just called it chocolate-flavored gingivitis. I caught him mid-scrub with my brush, as casual as a priest at mass.

I lifted my hands like, *Bro, that's mine.*
He looked at me like I was the freak.

My counterattack was simple. I bought a pink toothbrush—a little act of reconnaissance to mark my territory. No luck. He used that one, too. No shame. I stopped brushing at home—only at work. It was easier.

Yet, jobless as ever—in the middle of all these foul little quirks—he would write.

Benjamin would pen rebuttals to op-eds—dissertations, really—worthy of thesis accolades. Often mid-bender, he'd vanish into his corner, gulp a cocktail of codeine and Sudafed, nod off for a few hours, jolt awake from some nightmare, chop a line, sniff, and then snap back into consciousness to write. The joys of cocaine. It was like watching someone conduct a chemical symphony—down, up, down—until he emerged hours later with sharp, moving copy.

Brilliant stuff. I was jealous.

We urged him to submit to *The Atlantic* or *The Paris Review*, but he'd laugh. "Those smut rags? Not worthy of my words. They'd never understand."

Even his slippery contempt carried weight. With Benjamin, you got genius or lunatic—no in-between. A wiry rhythm he lived by, beats hammered out of his own volatility, dropped at random like flare guns, as if he needed the world to know he still existed.

I never caught all of his aphorisms, but one in particular stayed lodged in my head:

"There's no celestial fate scripting our meaning. We're flesh and nerves wrapped around a soul, and somewhere inside there's a drill—slow, steady—boring down until it strikes oil. Black and slick, beautiful in the way only danger can be, it rises through the eyes, ears, mouth, until it drowns us. When it does, we won't mind dying."

He may have stunk up the apartment, but those dips into the deep made you forget. For a moment, at least, he made you feel a little less shallow.

I suppose that's why patrons support the arts. The polished people—the tidy criers, the clean-fingered critics—fund the distance they need, while men like Benjamin pull the rest of us toward the parts of ourselves we'd rather not see.

Even now, I sometimes catch myself wondering: *Are you still drilling to find oil?*

But all oil comes with spills, and Benjamin was no exception.

By month three, the question began to drift through the apartment—quietly at first.

Then even from Jake. "So...Benjamin, have you found a place yet?"

Benjamin recoiled every time, drifting away with whatever excuse he could cobble up.

"It's a war out there, chip. Bunch of dumps," he'd mutter, coughing and pounding his chest like a Victorian widow recovering from consumption. "No luck."

December turned to January. January to February.
After five months of his freeloading, a fiscal reckoning arrived.

"Benjamin, so...we've got some bills. You could help since you've been here a bit," Isaac said—passively, carefully—as a statement and not a question. A question would've implied Benjamin was a roommate. A statement kept him a guest. Technically.

"Oh, I mean I can if you want me to. I just didn't realize I would, since, you know..." Benjamin paused. "It's not my place."

That line alone undid our philanthropy. We began to convene.

We took our strategy sessions to the local brick-oven pizza joint—our only safe place to avoid Benjamin's perpetual lurking.

"How the hell are we going to get him out of the apartment?" Jake asked. A clear sign his platonic infatuation was over.

As for the rest of us, Benjamin had become a stranger. No longer the wise elder who guided us cubs; no longer the guy who lifted mornings with a witty nothing or some old English saying from his mum. We only noticed him when an egg went missing from our labeled cartons, or when the milk ran suspiciously low.

Usually more mute than merciful, Mike snapped, "Just take his shit and leave it on the side of the road. I mean, he only owns a backpack, for Christ's sake. All this discussion is unnecessary."

We were all on board with that—except it wasn't possible.

Why, you ask?

Because here's the sick joke we didn't know at the time. In New York City, a squatter who's been living in your home for thirty days gains tenant rights. *Thirty days*. Not thirty years. Not thirty months. Thirty *little* days. After that, you can't just kick them out—you need a full legal eviction. Housing court. Paperwork. Judges. The whole bureaucratic parade.

"Yeah...my bad," Jake admitted.

He must've Googled it one night—probably between bouts of trying to get Benjamin to shut up whenever he broke into Hamlet's 'to be or not to be' monologue. But Jake hadn't told us sooner. Maybe he hadn't wanted to panic the herd. Maybe he'd still been hoping diplomacy might save us.

Regardless, once the law entered the chat, logic fled the building.

Our only weapon now was emotional warfare—the kind you deploy when your back's against the wall and kindness becomes a liability. And everyone knows logic never feels as good as emotion. So, you turn to chaos, because it holds you like a wire singeing with electric current. Benjamin, like most people, vibed off that. As if living in the flux of some coming-of-age myth were its own rite of passage.

But a rite of passage becomes a burden once everyone else has to carry it.
That's when it starts to rub people raw.
Like it did us.
Like it did Jake.

That's when I saw it—the shift.
Jake, the reluctant empath...
Jake, the guy who rescued spiders instead of killing them...
Jake, the baby-faced boy-genius with the soul of a preschool teacher...

He hardened.
Just a touch.

But enough to show that the world was finally pressing its thumb on him. Enough to show that whatever softness he'd been coasting on had reached its natural end. Jake looked at us, jaw set in a way I'd never seen, and said, "We'll force him out. We'll tell him we don't want him around."

That was the moment it became real.
A home-invasion of the spirit.
Our most passive-aggressive crusade yet: Project Kick Benjamin Out.

"We'll handle it tomorrow. Tonight, we enjoy the party," Jake said as we left the pizza joint—walking back toward what was, unbeknownst to Benjamin, his unofficial farewell party.

Which brings us back to the morning after that house party. The day dragged into late afternoon, and we were knee-deep in cleaning when Jake finally said, "Everyone—house meeting tonight at six. That includes you, too, Benjamin."

By evening, we descended into the basement in a half-circle, the single bulb above us flickering like it already knew what was coming.

Jake took the lead.

He told Benjamin—calmly, but with a firmness I'd never heard from him—that his time at the house was up.

"You've outstayed your welcome, Ben. We don't want you here anymore." He paused, then added, "Honestly...I don't even like you at this point."

Benjamin didn't flinch.
He didn't panic.
He didn't even blink.

"I live here," he said flatly. "I'm not leaving."

He'd said it like a lawyer delivering closing arguments—like the facts were so clearly on his side, this whole confrontation was a mere formality.

But beneath the calm, we knew what had happened.
He'd made himself immovable.
Not a guest. Not a friend.
A squatter with convictions.

A long stare lingered, with no one willing to take the next shot. Each of us stood stiffly, glancing sideways to see who would speak first. Somehow, we'd arranged ourselves like a lineup of aggression. Jake the strongest, then Jorge, then Mike, then Isaac—and me, Joe, tucked safely in the back.

The whole scene felt absurd. Ridiculous, even.

Benjamin hunched over, having just placed a battered library copy of *The Hobbit*—a 1980s paperback, I think—on the arm of his 'area,' the loveseat-turned-bed wedged in beside my basement room. Then, without ceremony, he reached beside him and lifted a thin yellow notepad, the kind with blue lines and a single bent corner. His personal sketchbook.

"Here—take this. Write down the reasons why I should leave. Be honest. I doubt you can write ten."

Jake rolled his eyes, then looked back at the rest of us. We all knew how stupid this was. Were we really about to draft a list of reasons Benjamin had been a bad guest?

A group exercise in squatter intervention?

The whole thing was asinine. Like writing a thank-you note to a burglar.

But Jake took the notebook anyway. We left Benjamin and headed upstairs to the kitchen.

Jake wrote with the pious certainty of a prophet. With each entry, his eyes would lift slowly from the page, locking on one of us for exactly three seconds—one...two...three—and then he'd nod, proud of his own wisdom. None of us could see what he was writing. The ritual was part exorcism, part execution.

Back to the pad. More scribbling. More bug-eyed glances. After fifteen minutes of solitary fury, Jake leaned back like a man who'd just drafted a constitution. He'd filled the whole Strathmore sheet—twenty-four reasons, neatly scrawled in slanted caps.

He declared, "I'm good here. Any other takers?"

No one moved.

I finally said it for everyone. "No."

Jake grinned, eager. "Benjamin, come up! We're doing this now."

His voice carried the smug anticipation of a man about to serve an eviction notice written in poetic bullet points.

We heard Benjamin shuffle off the loveseat. A thud echoed from the basement—he must've dropped the Tolkien paperback again—which made us all pause for one last breath before facing Benjamin for the final time.

He emerged slowly, climbing the stairwell with the reluctant dignity of a man headed to his own trial. He sat at the kitchen barstool, sluggish, face dry and withered from too many cigarettes. His elbows hit the counter. He dropped his jagged jaw into the cradle of his palms, and his cracked, near-bleeding lips drew a straight line between his two pinkies.

"Okay, well, let me start," Jake began. "Number one—"

"No, no. Let me read the bloody pad," Benjamin cut in. "It's my goddamn obituary, isn't it?"

It was pure Benjamin—he wasn't going to let Jake narrate his downfall. No, he'd do it himself, with theatrical flourish.

The interruption only made Jake seethe. This had become a duel—roommates be damned. The rest of us sat back, silent witnesses to the showdown.

Benjamin plucked the notepad from Jake's hands, smirking. "Thanks, chip."

Once a nickname full of flair and oddball affection, "chip" now landed like a toothache—sharp, persistent, and completely unwanted.

Benjamin rose from his stool like an understudy finally stepping into the lead. His head bobbed in approval of the moment. He gripped the corner of the bar like a courtroom lectern and looked down as if taking roll call.

"Number one," he announced, voice booming. "You are a nuisance to our living quarters—arrogantly eating our food and using our facilities without appreciation or compensation..."

He paused, scoffing.

"Arrogant?" he asked. "I bring life to this trepidation of filth and lack of original thinking." He lifted a hand to the heavens like a preacher mid-sermon, and then—his other arm dangling like a marionette on bad twine—pointed toward Jake with a limp, disdainful claw. "I just bought a dozen eggs. Free-range. USDA-fucking-approved. You know how much you love those, Jake."

For the next twenty minutes, Benjamin performed his rebuttal like it was scripture—line for line, reason for reason, without a moment of reflection. It was uncanny, as if God Himself were working him from the inside, a ventriloquist with a broken sense of mercy. Every accusation met an immediate counterargument.

Too quick. Too rehearsed. He wasn't hearing us; he was defending a myth.

And in that effort, I could see something begin to crack. The connection he'd thought he had to us—the brotherhood, the spark—had long since burned out. He looked suddenly wooden, like Pinocchio caught mid-lie, still insisting the truth was his to control.

All that posturing now seemed desperate. Hollow.

The magic was gone.

Still, he went on, volleying Jake's reasons with affected wit and lace-trimmed verbosity. What had started as an eviction turned into a debate. A battle of egos. A contest to see who was more articulate, more righteous, more intellectually indignant.

"Reason number four," Benjamin declared, punching the page like a courtroom stenographer. "'You feign artistic notoriety only to disguise your indolence *toward* securing an occupation.'"

He paused. Then—he laughed.

A real laugh. Two silver fillings sparkled under the kitchen light, relics from a different life. He leaned back, catching himself mid-wobble, one foot stepping back for balance just in time to avoid a collapse. Then—steadied—he leaned forward into Jake's face, eyes gleaming like a prize-fighter before the opening bell.

"Oh, how *incredible* this is," he hissed, his voice crawling with venomous glee. "You haughty, insolently deranged little piece of shit. *You*...criticize *me*?"

Then, the cruelty turned personal.

"You work at a fucking candy store."

The line hung in the air like a slap.

Context: Jake worked at a candy store—though he also tutored English on the side. A detail Benjamin omitted with surgical precision.

The crowd froze.

Benjamin, feeling the momentum shift, turned feral. The mask of charm fell. He began lashing out at the rest of us: liars, cowards, celibates. But it always circled back to Jake. That's where the venom lived.

"You're just pissed because you can't get laid!" he spat, pacing now, arms flailing. "God—you *wish* you could live like me."

What happened after that was blurry. The departure was—magnificently—unexpected.

No door slam. No tantrum. No last stand.

Instead, Benjamin showed us his truest self. He rushed downstairs and retrieved his one item of value—the backpack. His only possession. When he returned to the kitchen, there was something in his eyes—not rage, not pride, but a subtle plea.

He pulled his phone out and showed us his bank account. He had over $500,000.

In one last gasp, he tried to flip the script. "See that? Half a million. I've also got a *Matisse* in my parents' house in England. You guys are the joke. I don't give a damn if you kick me out. You're not pure anyway. You're a bunch of mouth breathers."

The room didn't react.
The reveal clarified everything.

He was privileged—surprisingly so.
Benjamin had been playing Bohemian the entire time.
Performing poverty.

Jake, unmoved, stood by the door. "Good for you," he said. "Now, get out."

Benjamin scanned the room one last time.
His eyes paused on each of us.
He wasn't looking *at* us—he was asking.
Asking for someone to say, *Stop. Wait. Let's talk more.*
But no one did.
We looked down.
He knew.
It was time to go.

"Fuck you," he muttered as he passed Jake, apparently still hoping for one last reaction.

"FUCK YOU!" Jake roared, slamming the door behind him.

Just like that, the spell snapped.

The sound ricocheted off the walls, echoing in a metallic ping before fading into a silence so full it felt sacred.

We held it.
A hush.
A moment of respect.
A farewell to arms.
A goodbye to Benjamin.

We looked at Jake. Then each other. No words.

We never heard from the opulent squatter again.

The Imposter of McIntire Hall

Break one rule, and the next one bends.
Not because you're reckless, but because you're curious.
You want to know how far life will let you go before it hits back.

We think the reckoning comes from an authority figure—a teacher, a lover, a cop. More often, it arrives without witnesses. Conscience keeps asking one question: *What if today's the day I'm caught?*

I've been asking myself that for nearly two decades. Let's go back to the night it began.

My college scandal.

Wheaton College lived in the sleepy town of Norton, Massachusetts—thirty, forty-five minutes from Boston or Providence—but far enough that we pretended the outside world didn't exist. I was a senior with four months left before graduation.

On Saturday nights, we turned boredom into mischief, convinced we were safe inside the bubble of a small liberal arts school. It was February. The snow still had fangs.

"I'm ready to get hammered!" Steve said, looking for something stupid to do.

"Yeaaaa, maaaan, let's make some memories we'll forget—yeehaaa!" Billy screeched, half laugh, half hyena.

Billy and Steve were frequent guests at Wheaton—hometown heroes from up north, enrolled at the University of Maine in Orono, a school with the same cold Saturdays but, as Billy put it, different 'babe quality.'

I wasn't chasing girls that night—I'd developed more of a taste for pranks. Water balloons, Dixie cups, Super Soakers... My credit card had the receipts, each with its own story. A rivalry had been simmering between me and two dormmates—fellow pranksters Sara and Betty—and the shenanigans had only escalated when our friend Kim had joined the chaos a couple weeks earlier.

Kim worked in student life—dry and droll without ever crossing into creepy. From a distance, she could've passed for a mid-40s administrator or a townie lurking in the campus crater we called the Dimple. She lived on the edge of student madness—near enough to watch it, never near enough to leave fingerprints.

A week earlier, Kim had let something slip. Sara and Betty had planned a girls' weekend in Providence. Their room would be empty. Kim didn't hand me anything. She didn't say what to do. She just smiled the kind of smile that said, *Do what you will.*

Naturally, I took full advantage.

At 3 a.m. Saturday, with help I won't name, we hauled the girls' mattresses through a back window and onto the dorm roof. I knew they'd be back the next day and couldn't wait to see their faces. By sunrise, the stunt felt like campus lore.

The girls were good sports about it. Annoyed, sure—but by Sunday evening, the mattresses were back where they belonged, the story already softening into something we'd retell at the lunch table at Emerson Dining Hall on Monday.

That scheme didn't cost me anything. No deans came knocking. No consequences followed. It was only later that I understood the lesson: *Pranks only linger when the target is a stranger.*

"Hey, how about we do something different?" I tested Billy and Steve.

"I'mmm doowwn fooor iiiiit allll, maaaan—yeeeaaah!" Billy screeched, his face purpled with strain.

Steve grinned. "Like what?"

"A prank."

At the time, Asher Roth's "I Love College" felt less like a song and more like permission. His ode to the frivolous was the soundtrack for a student body clinging to everything about to vanish. By the end of the song, he chants, "Freshman, Freshman—do something crazy, do something crazy."

That line stuck. And right then, I thought: *Why not the freshmen?*

I'd like to say the idea was mine that night. It wasn't. I'd seen it done three years earlier.

My freshman year, I played basketball. "Played" might be generous. I was a proud benchwarmer. Aside from 6 a.m. runs and late-night lifts, life as an athlete meant being surrounded by guys who knew grades didn't matter. They were there to ball and push the limits of campus authority.

One of my teammates was a guy named Riccardo.

Riccardo was the kind of snarky son of a bitch you wanted to punch. A total dickhead—but somehow, against your better judgment, you wanted him around.

Back in my freshman year, he was under investigation—already marked by the administration. Whatever he'd done had earned him weekend bans and a shifting list of restrictions, depending on who you asked.

One Saturday night, visibly drunk, Riccardo stumbled back across the campus border, pushing his luck. He spotted me from a distance and drifted over.

"Lee, come with me," he said.

We ended up in Gebbie Hall, senior territory.

Riccardo paused. "I'm trying to get a bag." By *bag*, he meant *weed*.

We knocked. No answer. The place was dark. Empty for the weekend.

"Well, this fucking sucks." He kicked the carpet like it owed him money. "Say...want to get into some trouble?"

"What do you have in mind?"

He grinned. "Wanna pull a prank?"

"Depends. What's the play?"

"Have you ever acted like an RA to get beer from freshmen?"

I hadn't.

Student Resident Advisors, or RAs, were upperclassmen hired to police dorm life. What I found odd was their willingness to trade weekends for so-called nobility, a clipboard with a whiff of power. You get 101 weekends in four years of college—yes, I did the math. Why forfeit 202 days of memories for one extra line on a résumé?

Beats me.

So, when Riccardo suggested we impersonate one, we walked into freshman territory. Underclassmen housing sat at the bottom of the hill. There were two dorms, Meadows East and McIntire Hall—relics with green linoleum and popcorn ceilings, places you endured so housing could improve later.

Riccardo laid out the plan. "The trick's simple. Knock, announce yourself, sound bored enough to be believable." He looked between the two towers. "Let's go to Meadows."

"We can't," I said. "I live there. They all know me. No one's buying me as an RA."

Riccardo paused, then snapped his fingers. "Then, McIntire it is."

The front door hung open—the college had never bothered fixing the hinge—so we slipped inside without a key.

Riccardo grinned. "To be the imposter," he said, slurring slightly, "you have to think like the imposter."

That made no sense. Still, I was curious.

I stood at the far end of the hallway—close enough to watch doors crack open, far enough off to stay unseen.

He knocked. "Open up," he said. "Surprise alcohol check. Student RA."

A freshman cracked the door. "Uh, hey...we don't have any."

An obvious lie—I could smell the buzz from where I stood.

"Okay, I gotta check," Riccardo said. "President of the college wants proof you kids aren't drinking tonight. And if you are, I gotta wri—te you up." He hiccupped on the word *write*.

The freshman squinted. "You're drunk."

"No, no, I'm not," Riccardo said. "Direct order from President Rucker."

The freshman hesitated, then stepped aside. "Fine. Take a look."

Riccardo disappeared into their room.

A minute later, I heard him lower his voice. "Well, well, well..." he repeated. "Looks like we got ourselves some fun juice."

Silence among the two underclassmen.

"I tell you what. How about I take these cans of golden courage, and we say they were never here?" His voice dropped further. "I'm doing you—a—favor."

Riccardo emerged seconds later with a thirty-rack of Bud Light.

The belligerent goofball supplied one more pearl of wisdom. "Booze ain't the way to go, boys. You wanna grow up to be like me when you're seniors."

"Thanks for the advice, man. Now, fuck off." The student slammed his door hard enough to nearly knock Riccardo backward, but the weight of the beer steadied him.

Riccardo giggled like a kid who'd stolen fireworks. He threw me a cold one. Night over.

I told Billy and Steve the Riccardo story. Naturally, three winters later, we reran the play.

We walked into McIntire expecting the same harmless gag—smooth, funny, easy. Nervous freshmen. Cheap beer. Clean exit.

We knocked on two doors.

The first opened to a sweet girl and her blasé friends. And by blasé, I mean they sat, looked, and spoke like they didn't care—while caring way too much about looking like they didn't care. No booze. Just sad souls working overtime to look sadder.

The second door was the mistake.

The occupant was a snotty blonde kid I recognized from the baseball team. Not that there weren't good players on the team, but this one wasn't one of them. His face was a field of freckles under bleached hair, Dennis the Menace come alive—pudgy cheeks you could blame on youth, and an expression caught somewhere between confused and pissed.

He opened the door and squinted at me. "What do you want?" he asked. "I don't know you."

"Well, sir," I said, slipping into Riccardo's old routine, "I'm a student RA—and tonight's your lucky night. We're conducting a random alcohol search. We need to check your room."

He stared at me. Billy and Steve stayed quiet.

"Really?" he asked. "Show me your IDs."

"What? Why?" I asked.

"There's a stamp on IDs," he said, "that proves you're a RA."

Damn it. I hadn't known about that.
Since Riccardo's night, Wheaton must have tightened things up.

Steve jumped in, smooth as ever. "Oh—never mind. Looks like your room's all set."

Billy grunted. "Our mistake. Have a good night."

"Show me your IDs!" the kid snapped. "Or are you phonies stealing beer from freshmen?"

He reached for my shirt.

"Don't touch me," I said, swatting his hand away. "You don't get to check me."

I should've stopped there. If I'd walked away, it would've been over. But my senioritis got the better of me, and he got under my skin.

I stuck it to him. "Don't be such an arrogant prick."

"Prick?" he echoed. "We'll see who's the prick when I report this to my *actual* RA."

Right then, a figure appeared at the end of the hallway.

"What's going on here?" the RA asked. "Why's everyone yelling?"

I looked at the stairwell. "Run!" We booked it.

"Get them!" the kid yelled. "Imposters!"

We tore through McIntire and out into the cold—from lower campus to upper—before collapsing in my dorm, out of breath and half-panicked.

Mischief has a way of calling you back. It only feels like fun if no one gets hurt—though sometimes, even when someone does, we still laugh.

And that night, Steve, Billy, and I laughed.
Hell, we laughed until there were no more laughs to give.

The following morning Steve and Billy drove back to Maine. As they drove off, I thought it was over. Another stupid story for later. A harmless homage, I told myself—just part of the good old college try.

Then, Monday came. My roommate Bob pulled me aside one morning.

Bob was an editor for the school newspaper, *The Wheaton Wire*—closer to small-town gossip than *The New York Times*, though we treated it the same. It came out monthly, and when it did, it was campus scripture. Get your name in print, and you were famous—even the Norton townies stayed plugged in.

Bob fixed me with a death stare. "Dude," he said, "they're running a story about you."

My coffee went cold in my hand. I didn't drink it.

Bob leaned in. "Man," he said, "I'm talking about the other night. You—the imposter of McIntire Hall."

Bob must have heard me retelling the story that night—his room was right next to mine. We'd been loud. Too loud. I wondered who else had heard.

"They're trying to find who did it," he said. "There's a whole description—'Blonde-haired male with two dark-haired men posing as student RAs, breaching college code. If you know their whereabouts, please inform Susan Lynn, Dean of Student Life.'"

"Bob, you have to stop them!" I said. "Don't let them print that. For real, this is bad. I can't get kicked out of school for this."

"I tried," he said. "That made people suspicious. Honestly, we shouldn't hang out for a bit. Bad enough I have brown hair—they might assume I was in on it."

"Fuck," I said. "What happens if someone tells on me?"

"I don't know, man. But they're pissed. Apparently, the kid you pranked is some rich asshole from Denver, and he told his parents. Now, they're calling it harassment. The school wants to make an example. It's blown up." Bob was breathing heavily—I could tell he felt for me.

"Did you tell anyone else?" I was scrambling.

"Yeah...a few people. But don't worry—no one we know is gonna tell." He shrugged. "You know how it is here. Everything's a big controversy until it blows over."

Defining words, I thought.

For a few days, I was safe. Then, the paper came out. Thursday morning, everyone—and I mean *everyone*—was talking about "the imposter." The great prankster mystery.

Sara—one of the victims of my mattress joke—sat down next to me at breakfast. "Hey, did you hear about this *imposter*? Hilarious. I remember seniors pulling that when we were freshmen. But I guess they're cracking down now. I wonder who it is?"

She stabbed a grape and wedged it into a slice of honeydew. I said nothing. Just rolled a hard-boiled egg on the table and peeled it in silence.

"Hey, are you okay?"

I played it coy. "I'm fine. Why?"

"I don't know—you seem quiet," she pressed.

She was right. Something in me had slipped.

She leaned closer. "Wait...Joe...no. You're the imposter. You did it."

I looked away. My stomach tightened into a nervous smile. My heart picked up.

"Oh, no—it's okay," she said softly. "I won't say a word."

Now, she was implicated, too—like Bob before her. I left my tray and walked out of the dining hall. Sara stayed seated.

On the way to class, I was early. I was always early now.
I thought staying ahead of the crowd would keep me invisible.

It didn't.

Even on an empty campus, I felt the eyes.

I drifted toward a bench parked too close to the sidewalk, like it had washed ashore and stuck. No student ever used it. Kim did. Her morning ritual—watching the campus wake up, nodding hello before the first classes began.

As I passed, trying to stay invisible, I saw Kim sitting beside a woman with giant-rimmed glasses and shoulder pads sharp as verdicts. I knew it was Dean Lynn. She didn't just enforce rules. She liked the fear that made them work.

Oddly enough, Kim adored Dean Lynn. Or at least Kim understood her. Kim played the good angel—present, patient, trusted by students.

Dean Lynn played the devil, with the final word and the fear that made things stick.

I looked at my phone—the universal sign of being busy, rushed, late for something.

"Oh, this is Joe Lee—he's swell," Kim's voice carried from thirty feet away. "Have you met him?"

"Good morning, Joe. Nice to meet you," Dean Lynn said.

"You as well," I mumbled.

"In a rush? Classes haven't started yet," Dean Lynn asked, her lemon-tart lips puckering with the kind of judgment that makes you confess before you know your crime. She didn't need proof. She needed *pressure.*

"I need to finish some biochemistry homework. Thought it was due later, but it's actually in fifteen minutes. I'm freaking out," I lied.

Dean Lynn stayed stoic. She'd caught a whiff of smoke, and I prayed I could move before it settled.

"Oh, well, get going," Kim said.

I nodded to Dean Lynn and excused myself. It felt like staring down my future.

Coming clean might have relieved everything. But one childhood lesson in guilt by association taught me this: *Honesty is a luxury when the punishment is already decided.*

As the morning's biochemistry lecture droned on, my mind wandered back to that lesson.

I was twelve. Seventh grade. My middle school had bought new hexagon lunch tables, state of the art, with latches on both sides. Pull one, nothing. Pull both at once, and the whole thing snapped upright, like half a table trying to become a wall.

In schools, the warning comes before the crime. Tell students not to do something, and that's when they get their best ideas. So, the administration held a forum and handed us the blueprint: *Don't pop the tables—do it, and you'll get a white slip.*

A white slip wasn't catastrophic—basically a demerit—but at Lewiston Middle School, even one meant ineligibility for the annual field trip to the city's ice rink. Break the rule, and you were cast out—the iron fist of watery hot dogs and the almighty Zamboni.

So, I sat at a table I shouldn't have been at, beside kids I barely knew—the kind you nod to but never follow into trouble. It was the last empty chair at lunch. One kid beside me, and another across from him, started fiddling with the table's latches.

Then, I felt it, the table gyrating.

The thrill wasn't in popping the table. The thrill was in popping it and pushing it back down before anyone noticed. Every few minutes, once the lunch monitor passed, the pop-and-push resumed. My chicken fingers rattled across the tray like dice in a cup.

Then, the cup spilled.

The table popped, and no one pushed it back down. A safety lock clicked. The towering half-hexagon jutted upward like an accusation.

Of course, the lunch monitor was the worst kind of enforcer: Mr. Cherry, the history teacher—rumpled button-down oxford, woolly bow tie, permanently stuck in another decade.

He hauled us to his classroom to write us up.

I stood there in front of his eighth graders, a deliberate mockery of composure, fighting the urge to crack. I failed. I cried.

One girl gave me the look: *It's okay. It's not that big a deal.*

Mr. Cherry didn't care. No sentiment, no sympathy.

Later, my homeroom teacher heard what had happened. She knew my nature. I wasn't that kid back then. Mrs. Bleakney spoke to Cherry off the record, and with her vouching, the white slip was rescinded. I went to the rink, drank cocoa, and skated for hours.

That middle-school episode was tame beside this Wheaton scandal. That had been a white slip. This was my life—and I had no idea whether the verdict would be suspension or expulsion.

If Dean Lynn had said, "This ends with a fifty-dollar fine," I would've agreed on the spot. But silence left me with the one thing rules without consequences always offer: *Might.*

Might is torture. Punishment ends. *Might* never does.

A month passed. Talk of the "imposter" thinned.

That's when I saw Kim.

An early riser, especially on Sundays. She spotted me at the window and waved. I waved back and cracked the window as she approached. The sky was nearly blue, except for one gray cloud hanging in the distance.

"Gorgeous day, huh?" she asked, crouching slightly to meet the window.

"Amazing. Just that one cloud messing it up."

"If you hold your finger up, it disappears." She demonstrated.

"What are you up to?" I asked.

She started rummaging in her bag. "I've been up for hours working."

"On what?"

"Putting up flyers. Still looking for that 'imposter'." She leaned closer.

"Flyers?" I echoed.

"Here. Take one." She pulled a neon pink sheet from her bag—bold black type screaming accusation, the whole night reduced to a headline.

I looked past her hand and saw them everywhere—tree trunks, benches, dorm doors, windows. Neon pink, polka-dotted across campus.

I thought: *Wheaton's deans aren't administrators anymore.*
They were bounty hunters with letterhead—and I was very much alive.

"They'll never find 'em." Kim paused.

My throat tightened.

"Public Safety sent a follow-up email to RAs and staff with a description." She read aloud—casual, like a grocery list: "Blonde male. Slim build. Green or blue eyes. Seen wearing a cream-colored Ralph Lauren oxford." She laughed again. "See? Could be anyone."

On the chair behind me hung the cream oxford I wore every weekend.

Then, half-joking, half-not, Kim added, "Lynn and I were laughing the other day when you walked by. She said chasing the imposter felt like a wild goose chase."

Kim hesitated.

"After you left, she said you fit the profile."

I tried to laugh. It sounded fake. Kim noticed.

"Joe," she said gently. "Do you know who did it?"

There it was. A lifeline. Or a trap.

I looked up at the sky and raised a finger, blotting out the lone gray cloud.

I said, "Whoever it was has punished himself enough."

Kim studied me.

"Yeah," she said finally. "I'm sure he has."

She sighed.

"Between us," she said, "something else came up this weekend. Lynn's already onto it—vandalism. A hate crime splattered across a student's dorm door. You'll read about it in the *Wire*."

"That's terrible," I said.

Kim's mouth twitched. Not a smile. A decision.

"Alright," she said. "Gotta go."

As she walked away, I watched her drop the last of the flyers into a trash can.

Maybe that's how it works. The guilt stays. The pink fades.

Pardon the Parrots and Their Banana Peels

Medicine is a theater of gatekeeping. Degrees decide who belongs. But I had none of those walnut-framed meal tickets on the wall. I was the last man you'd expect to be writing manuscripts about in vitro fertilization.

My entry into IVF wasn't deliberate. It was 2011. I was between jobs, crashing on a friend's couch in Bridgeport, Connecticut, trying to claw my way back to New York City.

The job found me on a late-night Craigslist scroll.
The listing read: *Medical Writer at a Fertility Center.*

The description was vague, dense with jargon and impossible qualifications. All I had was a college degree and a Harvard-adjacent research assistantship in a stem cell lab. I'd helped on a paper that landed in *Cell*, one of the big biology journals—prestigious in certain circles, but I had nowhere near the eleven years it takes to become a fertility specialist.

The path into reproductive endocrinology and infertility is anything but simple: four years of medical school, four years of residency, three years of fellowship. Those years weren't mine.

I knew how improbable it was that I'd get hired.
Still, I thought, *Why not apply?*
If I got the gig, I'd learn my usual way—by bingeing YouTube videos.

I got an interview.
I bluffed my way through it.

"You aren't really qualified," Dr. Gibson, the CEO, said.

"Tell you what," I said. "Knock ten percent off the salary. Give me two months. If I can't make something happen, fire me."

By *something*, I meant *publications*.

He leaned over his desk, stared me in the eyes, then smirked. "You start next week."

I nodded like I belonged.

Writing was only the visible part of the job. The rest was running the research arm of a private practice—regulatory paperwork, consent forms, turning clinical data into scientific stories. Citable material meant better patient care and a stronger clinic reputation.

Within a month, a journal accepted our first manuscript.
Within three months, two more followed.

Turns out a bluff isn't always a lie.

Most people don't understand that early publication success wasn't normal.

Placement played a part—the setting favored us.

Dr. Gibson wasn't running a hospital. A private practice is closer to a tech startup than a university lab—leaner, faster, less precious about titles. While academic institutions trudged at a glacial pace, we ran our research arm like a burn-the-candle operation. Output came fast, even if the establishment frowned.

Timing mattered.

In the early 2010s, IVF wasn't mainstream. No influencers. No podcasts. Assisted reproductive technology was evolving fast. Genetic testing, cryostorage, new treatment strategies—everything moving faster than most physicians could absorb. It felt like a golden era, a window when the field was exploding with publishable material. Research wasn't treasure you hunted for. It was driftwood washing ashore—someone just had to pick it up and carve it into something real.

In a world of protocol, polish, and pedigree, Dr. Gibson made a rebel's choice. He hired me, a mill-town kid from Maine with no MD or PhD. In the medical community, that broke tradition. We both knew the move was heresy.

But Dr. Gibson was entering his own transformative era. He wanted a legacy that reshaped a field, not one that fattens bank accounts. He came from a disappearing strain of physicians who believed medicine carried a civic and intellectual duty beyond clinic walls. He still carried that academic impulse. Publish or perish—not for applause, but for correction. To leave something behind. Maybe even a quiet claim to immortality.

Even if he rarely said it aloud, he knew he'd never get the research he wanted from colleagues who treated inquiry like extra credit. He needed an ally who wasn't jaded by the system—someone unindoctrinated, someone scrappy, someone who didn't know the invisible rules well enough to fear breaking them.

My naïveté became his opening.

Whether it was his calling or my luck, our shared appetite for output pulled us into a current neither of us fully understood. And against every expectation, it *fucking* worked.

From my gargoyle perch in a windowless cubicle, I cranked out spreadsheets, pivot tables, and SPSS analyses—statistical software, for the blissfully unaware. Dr. Gibson, between patients, guided my editorial scalpel, fixing noun-verb agreement and slicing away dangling modifiers before a paper went to print.

Through manuscript after manuscript, we built a reputation—a tiny team landing outsized results. Soon, we were known as a one-two knockout in controlled ovarian stimulation.

After a couple of years, Dr. Gibson urged me to pitch research projects to everyone—physicians, nurses, embryologists, therapists, and even the IT guy. Anyone who so much as blinked toward curiosity. We assumed enthusiasm was contagious, that people would feel the same jolt of *we're building something here.* For a moment, there was heat. Nods. Excitement.

Then the cooling.
Then the quiet.
Then the ghosting.

The same voices that said "Let's do it!" evaporated when follow-through was required. When I nudged them later, thinking maybe they'd forgotten, I'd get the classic refrain:

"I already work too much. I have a life outside the office, you know?"

That's when it hit me—this was a medical practice first, and my little research department rode in the back seat. Anything I started was Cinderella before the ball: useful, invisible, and stuck scrubbing floors. No one wanted to gamble on her while she was still covered in ash. But once the glass slipper fit—once the data looked polished enough to show off—everyone swore they'd believed in her all along.

It wasn't about clinical value. It was about asking exhausted physicians, nurses, and embryologists to tack one more task onto a twelve-hour day.

Early on, I took it personally. By year five, I'd smartened up. I knew my place in the charade—the lone research hand with ink-stained fingers. No feelings hurt. Output was its own reward.

What I didn't expect was how quickly indifference turns to interest when the spotlight arrives.

Our manuscripts started gaining national attention, and suddenly the same research once dismissed as "IVF minutiae" became prime currency. I could feel it before anyone said anything—the way conversations tightened when I walked into rooms where I used to be invisible.

Then, the glow hit.

Reality television drifted into medicine. Cameras showed up in clinics. Egg-freezing became clickbait. Tears turned into storylines for future trust-fund babies. In the decade that followed, IVF became a pop-culture accessory, lumped in with nose jobs and Birkin bags.

Once the spotlight arrived, the tone inside the clinic changed.

Collegial praise hardened into academic warfare. Our data wasn't just data anymore; it was marketing collateral. Research became a hot commodity. Physicians wanted clips, screenshots, citations—anything to polish a personal brand.

To understand what came next, you have to see the machinery behind the myth.

Medical publishing runs on two currencies: manuscripts and abstracts. Think of manuscripts as the full film and abstracts as the trailer. Same story, different scale.

Manuscripts are long, peer-reviewed studies—full clinical papers in journals like *Fertility and Sterility* and other top-tier outlets. A diploma on the wall is one piece of paper. Twenty, forty, a hundred manuscripts—that's a cathedral of clout, brick by brick, publication by publication.

Abstracts are short summaries presented at conferences and printed later in journal supplements. Useful. Respectable. Sometimes influential. But abstracts don't get you tenure.

Then, there's authorship—the quiet bloodsport of medical publishing.

Unlike a book with one or two names, research papers parade out half a dozen or more. Order matters. It's hierarchy written into the byline. First, second, and last carry weight. Everyone in the middle? "Co-authors." A generous term for anyone whose main contribution was hearing the idea out loud once.

But no one ever says, "I was a co-author." Not at dinner parties. Not on dates. Not on LinkedIn. The "co-" gets dropped like an embarrassing middle name.

That's where things in my position got interesting. As colleagues started looping themselves into projects—mostly after the fame monster began circling—they scrambled for authorship. I became their de facto editor, which is a polite way of saying I rewrote a lot of papers, sometimes from the ground up.

For years, the machine kept running.
But every machine has a choke point.

Names on a page decide careers, podium invites, Instagram relevance—first picked, last picked, or not picked at all. A pecking order as old as gym class: captains calling names while everyone else studies the floor.

Dr. Gibson understood the landmines buried in all that "teamwork." Authorship wars destroy practices; they end friendships. He wanted no part of refereeing egos. So—in another move that still feels unbelievable—he handed me the reins.

I decided whose names went on papers, and in what order. If anyone protested, Dr. Gibson could shrug and say, "Joe decided, not me."

Naturally, since I had no MD or PhD, my name rarely appeared first. You give a little, you get some back. Whatever kept the machine moving, I'd do it.

And if anyone complained? Easy—blame it on me.

Which brings us to the real dirty secret about medical publishing: abstracts are the most fun. They're your golden ticket to conferences.

Conferences are hosted by professional societies that rely on research to guide best practice. For us, that group was the American Society for Reproductive Medicine—ASRM. The name became shorthand. Nobody said, "I'm going to the fertility conference." They said, "I'm going to ASRM."

You get the drift.

Abstracts are submitted, reviewed, and ranked. Then, you either get the axe or the green light—scheduled for a Poster or an Oral Presentation.

Orals are the prize—the handful chosen from thousands, the talks that put you on a national stage with nothing but slides and a microphone. If you think athletes are competitive, you've never watched doctors jockey for ten minutes of fluorescent light and a captive audience forced to hear your findings without interruption. That's the big leagues.

What's funny is that abstract counts supposedly don't matter to the gods of reproductive medicine. The intelligentsia insist they're meaningless.

One senior doctor told me, "Abstracts aren't real publications."

Except they are. Printed. Indexed. Archived forever. They are easy to belittle because they're easy to ignore—until a reporter needs a headline. The moment CNN, NBC, or *The New York Times* spun one into breaking news, the "worthless" abstract became currency overnight.

In the middle of that contradiction, I became the guy behind the curtain—the one shaping the words our clinic recited in conference halls and, somehow, on *Good Morning America*. My reputation seeped through convention centers—across rival practices, institutions, and biotech firms. People wanted their names beside mine.

And I delivered—more than they expected, more than they admitted.

If anything, the rising recognition pushed me into a strange but formidable role. I found myself quietly telling physicians how to practice medicine. The data we published shaped protocols, guided decisions, and corrected errors—subtly, but undeniably.

It still tickles me when someone mistakes me for a doctor. Once a pharma rep shook my hand and said, "Doctor, your work is incredible."

I smiled and dropped the line I'd perfected for moments like that: "No, I'm not a doctor. I just write research papers that tell doctors how to doctor."

Excuse me if the stack of papers went to my head. Cockiness wasn't a strategy—it was a side effect. I didn't yet know how to behave in that world, what passed for humor and what crossed an invisible line. What I thought was harmless charm soured in the wrong ears.

Dr. Gibson caught wind of it and pulled me aside—not angry, but not warm either. "Loose lips sink ships," he warned.

No kidding.

As practice notoriety grew, so did internal patrol. More gatekeepers arrived as the practice grew, and with them a renewed zeal for enforcing the rules—written and otherwise. The higher my profile rose, the more glory-snatchers leaned over the curtain, squinting at my résumé, sniffing for the pedigree that wasn't there.

"How did this guy get here?" they'd ask.

Suspicion I'd dodged for years started circling again, this time with teeth. Doubt entered the room. Skeptics began performing the little rituals that protect status.

First came the passive-aggressive claims of "presence equals contribution." Physicians informed me—straight-faced—that simply being in the building meant they deserved authorship. Not writing. Not reviewing. Not analyzing. Presence. As though clinic hours were the same as research.

Sure, they'd contributed to the datasets—though so had the nurses, the receptionist, the embryology team, and sometimes the guy who fixed the printer. But in their minds, an M.D. alone turned oxygen into authorship.

Then came the territorial nonsense. A physician once pulled me aside to say he "owned" a topic. Owned it—as though biology were land you could homestead. His argument: if anyone in the practice ever published on that subject again, his name should appear, whether he lifted a finger or not.

When I published a paper in that category without him, he lost his mind—as if we'd desecrated sacred reproductive scripture. I can only assume he believed in academic osmosis, that without his brilliance seeping into my fingertips, I had no right to touch a keyboard.

How careless of me to forget my place.

The same little power plays kept coming. This time from physicians who went rogue, trying to write manuscripts without me—a kind of academic cosplay, all swagger and no syntax. These weren't collaborations; they were auditions, bids to impress Daddy Gibson, who, to their irritation, trusted me with the work.

The younger physicians were the most cunning.
They whispered about me in hallways like conspirators.

The irony was that I heard every word.

By then, there was institutional crossover—unusual for a private practice, but, as you know, Dr. Gibson ran things his own way. Residents and medical students from nearby academic programs rotated through our halls under the physicians' supervision—and, occasionally, mine. Whenever someone tried to cut me out, it was the trainees who tipped me off.

One trainee chirped, "She said not to include you, but I am."

Trainees learn early to play the game—to align with whoever can move their careers an inch. They have to. They weren't about to burn bridges with the guy deciding whose name landed on the next paper. Still, they were confused about my role—first assuming I'd trained like them, then ignoring it as long as their names made the author list, later citing those same papers as proof I must have known what I was doing.

Once, a resident whispered, "But...didn't our journal club review a paper Joe co-wrote?"

An attending sneered, "He doesn't know the medicine. He's not a medical doctor like us."

True. I wasn't in the operating room. I wasn't diagnosing ovarian torsion. That wasn't my lane. But I was shaping the *fucking* literature they leaned on to stay current.

Sorry. Lost my cool there.

That "You don't have an MD" jab always hit something tender—a feud between me and the version of myself I never became. Those digs weren't just insults; they were reminders. Sharp ones. Because it wasn't that I'd never considered becoming a doctor. I'd tried.

I wasn't good enough.

I took the Medical College Admission Test—the MCAT. Bombed it twice.

No one knew. That was a private humiliation I carried for years.

I tried the GRE, too, the gateway to PhD programs. Same result.

All I had was this little writing shtick. My only leverage. I clung to it. A chip formed around it. Oppression—real or imagined—makes you defiant before you know it.

So, when someone tossed the "no-MD" dagger my way, it hit deeper than they knew.

Because I was bitter. Maybe I still am.

Eventually, the pressure reached Dr. Gibson. No more looking the other way. He engineered just enough harmony to keep the band from mutiny. He couldn't cut me from the work, so he left me off the guest list when gala invitations started arriving—black-tie celebrations, doctors-only soirées. Nothing in my inbox.

Allies would text me: *Why aren't you here?*
I'd reply: *Couldn't make it. Had other plans.*

Going along with the hierarchy wasn't malicious. Just optics. I still called the shots, but each year, the room felt a little less like mine. Dr. Gibson, for better or worse, had to keep up appearances with the other attendings. I didn't blame him.

Well, that's a lie.

Sometimes it hurt. Paralegals, assistants, vice presidents—you know the feeling. That pause in the middle of a task when you wonder, *Does anyone even notice what I'm doing anymore?*

For me, the ache wasn't status. It was realizing no amount of work—no data, no papers, no talks—would quiet the doubters. At one point, I crossed four hundred publications. Still, it didn't matter. I was needed, but not always wanted. Praise felt conditional. Silence felt strategic.

If any doctor bristles at that—relax. No one is at fault here. The system bruises us differently.

Some of them borrowed a quarter-million dollars to buy a ticket onto the field. I answered a Craigslist ad and landed on the same bench. It isn't strange that people guarding that investment didn't want to be second-guessed by someone walking the same halls. "Ostracized" is too strong, but there was a polite boxing-out. Professional courtesy with a moat.

From my vantage point, I saw things the rest of the room wouldn't. Some of the most endorsed names struggled with the work. They never knew it. Why would they? People like me cleaned up after them—quietly, reliably, invisibly.

You know the type. The fixer. The closer. The one who stays late. Being the street rat has its own small paradise. I may not meet the standards the higher-ups worship, but I get the satisfaction of carrying the load. And that, in its own way, is prestige.

For a long time, I thought the rest—degrees, titles, stacks of papers—made prestige permanent. A Wednesday coffee break cured me of that illusion. I mentioned I was heading to Costa Rica. Dr. Bearse, an attending, overheard and smiled—not bitter, not jealous. Just tired from procedures.

"I wish I'd done something like that," she said, peeling off her gloves. "I never took an excursion. Just college, med school, residency, fellowship, kids...then the rest."

She wasn't complaining. She was remembering.

That's what sacrifice becomes—the quiet hope you chose correctly. We all want someone to say the path was worth it. But no one really knows. Not Dr. Bearse. Not me. Not anyone.

Had I walked the prescribed route—school, residency, white-coat coronation—I would've inherited an identity I'd spend a lifetime defending. I couldn't live like that. I'd feel trapped.

Failure might have been the only luck I ever got. It left me untethered. It let me steal the keys when the gatekeeper wasn't looking—not to treat patients, not to impersonate a doctor, just to bypass permission culture. And if I ever wanted to walk away, I could—owing no one an explanation.

Still, in the quiet after a manuscript acceptance, the old disdain crept back—the writer's disease that turns every achievement into a reminder of what it might have been, had you chosen another path. A decade in medicine—or anywhere—makes you wonder whether the work chose you, or you chose it.

That's when I needed a reminder only youth could give—the students and residents rotating through our clinic. Their summer rotation had become a year-round assembly line of young minds lured by the promise of padding their CVs.

Each spring, when abstract-submission season hit, the trainees kept a faint spark alive. Every new cohort injected fresh blood into the sprint. We were comrades for a moment, racing under the same invisible timekeeper called *Deadline.*

Then, one season, someone appeared who set the whole thing on fire. His name was Oscar.

Oscar was a six-foot-six medical student behemoth—all elbows and enthusiasm—who barreled into our practice like he'd been shot out of a cannon. Bulging eyes, rapid-fire speech, crusted lips, and a gangly stomp that made you nervous for the floorboards.

He had a streak of white in his hairline—some genetic quirk, poliosis or whatever it's called. You'd think it was premature aging, but it had been destined to go white since birth. It flashed when he talked, like a lightning bolt begging for attention.

Oddities aside, he was pure-grade genius. Oscar seemed to have swallowed every season of *Jeopardy!*—Civil War trivia, half-digested quantum physics, why bitcoin would never work, and a sermon about Charlie Chaplin being the greatest actor who ever lived.

Ask how he knew, and he'd shrug, dead serious. "You pick things up here and there."

A brainiac, yes—but with one undeniable flaw: his feet.

Not in a fetish way. He just refused to wear shoes or socks. He'd sit barefoot at his desk, that white streak falling into his face while he explained the hormonal intricacies of IVF, picking lint from between his toes.

Then, he'd roll it between his fingers like a tiny football. Sometimes, he'd flick it. Sometimes, he'd hold it like a relic. Sometimes—I swear to God—he'd eat it.

Disgusting? Of course. But after a while, the shock dulls. When your mind runs a mile above the crowd, weirdness is the cover charge.

None of it bothered me—though others gagged at his fungal exhibitions. I saw something else: unfiltered energy, reckless earnestness, the spark I used to carry before politics and those forgotten gala invitations sanded me down. There was a purity to him. I wanted to protect it. Maybe light my own back up. And for a golden stretch, we made a hell of a team.

Like every abstract season, we started six months out. Then came the quiet interlude—the stretch after submission, when ASRM judged, accepted, denied, and assigned presenters.

By April, we were burning midnight oil—pruning, tightening, shaving word counts, sharpening the take-home message, slotting each piece into the right category. No dullness. No filler.

With Oscar beside me and the rest of the practice humming, we produced more abstracts than any season before. Oscar alone submitted ten. A record. I'd never seen one person generate that much medical writing—with his own stats—in a single sprint.

After we hit submit, Oscar celebrated by cracking open a can of something that looked like green sludge siphoned from an Arizona muffler.

"Want a dolma?" he asked.

"A what?"

Grape leaves stuffed with rice. Of course, Oscar had them at midnight on a random Wednesday after submitting abstracts.

Months later, the results came back.
Twenty-five abstracts accepted. Another banner year.
Oscar? Nine on his own. Stellar.

Then, the curveball. A new category: Prize Paper. Maybe because the conference was in Hawaii and they needed extra pizzazz. And who snagged Oral Presentation Number One? You guessed it.

Oscar.
Our grape-leaf-munching, toe-picking savant.

In the months before the conference, I drilled the trainees on their talks—public speaking, verbal tics, pacing, the difference between sounding polished and sounding like directions barked at the DMV.

You think I'm joking. I'm not. We took it seriously.

By any given conference week, it all felt ceremonial. The talks were recitals, polished and predictable. My budding physicians in their suits and dresses, ready for the big day, and me in the front row like a chaperone—listening not for brilliance, but for lapses. If one froze, I'd toss a softball question during Q&A, just enough to steady the room and get them offstage clean.

Then, the tempo would shift. Sessions started at 7:30 a.m.; by mid-afternoon, it was happy hour.

I had company approval to spend freely. Everyone else lived on thin stipends. As conference lead, I covered meals, drinks, and the quiet courting of collaborators or students who might one day join us. It worked. It also attracted moochers.

It wasn't unusual to hear things like:
"Can I jump in your Uber?"
"What are your plans for lunch?"
"Joe, can I put this drink on your tab?"

To be clear, the trainees weren't funded by us. They rotated through our clinic, but were paid by their institutions, and those stipends were razor thin.

At boarding time for Hawaii, it was no different for Oscar.
He shuffled past me, chewing a protein bar.

"You grab that outside the terminal?" I asked.

"No way," he said. "Walgreens. Five dollars. Why pay ten?"

There it was—economic philosophy in one sentence.

Earbuds in. Tray tables up.
Bon voyage. Hawaii.

The island greeted us the way only Hawaii could—humid air, salt in the breeze, parrots screeching from the palms like they owned the deed to Honolulu. They were everywhere, flashing green and red across the sky, dive-bombing between hotels and lampposts.

Dr. Gibson couldn't resist. "Look at those birds—'Polly want a cracker.'"

Our group of twenty—attendings, fellows, residents, and me—half-smiled, then peeled off in different directions, planning to regroup later for dinner.

The night before a conference isn't celebration. It's staging. Sake, sashimi, and quiet panic. Everyone pretends to relax while silently counting abstracts and swallowing stage fright.

The waiters kept refilling glasses like they were administering last rites.

The night ended when the owner of the fusion place burst into our private room and announced, "Hey, we're out of booze. Time to go."

Outside, Oscar staggered off like a lost puppy, announcing he was going to walk the two miles back to his Airbnb.

Dr. Gibson and I exchanged a look, then flagged a cab.

I tossed the driver a twenty. "Keep the change."

Oscar piped up, "No—I'll take the change."

I sighed, pulled out another twenty, and slapped it into his hand.

"Use this to get to the conference tomorrow. Don't be late."

Monday morning was brutal. Hungover, I still made it to the convention center by 7:00 a.m., checking in with colleagues and students slated to present later in the day.

Everyone was there...except Oscar.

I started with a soft text: *where are you?*
By 7:15, soft turned to panic. I called. No answer.
Texted again: *Dude? Answer!*

Finally, at 7:25, he replied: *On the way, running.*

Running?

Meanwhile, the room filled with doctors, PhDs, pharma reps—four hundred people settling into their seats, waiting for Oscar's big moment.

Dr. Gibson waved me over, pressure tightening around his jaw. "Where the hell is Oscar?"

"He's on his way...I think."

The murmur grew, along with the ritual peacocking—name-dropping, chest-thumping, promises about grant money nobody had secured yet.

7:27 a.m.

Dr. Gibson leaned in. "You might need to step in."

It wouldn't have been the first time someone bailed on a presentation. In those rare disasters, I'd jump in—I knew the research front to back—but stage fright hits differently when you're drafted with thirty seconds' notice. I stepped forward, ready to take the bullet.

Then, the conference room doors exploded open.
Oscar entered.
The second coming.

Sweat streamed down his face. His tie dangled like Rodney Dangerfield looking for respect. And—though no one else seemed to notice—he was wearing white sport socks with dress shoes.

I pushed through the crowd and grabbed his arm. "Where the fuck have you been?"

"Hungover. Overslept. Ran here." Still gasping, he added, "Why'd you make me drink so much last night?"

The accused always rewrites the crime.

Then, like the diva he was, he asked, "Can you get me some water and a banana?"

I fetched both.

He gulped the water.
The banana slid into his suit pocket like a yellow pistol he'd fire later.

Then, something shifted.

Maybe it was the power of the podium, but as Oscar strutted down the aisle, he moved like the Liberace of Laparoscopy—cutting through the leering eyes, ready to set the stage on fire.

And that *motherfucker* delivered.

Too polished for a man who'd been half-dead minutes earlier. That's the hangover miracle. When the cards are down, pressure melts away. Nothing matters. You land a triple axel you didn't know you had.

Oscar did exactly that.
Perfect tens across the board.

Doctors leaned forward, eyes bright with that we're-witnessing-genius sheen. For a moment, they forgot sperm and egg were required for life. They marveled at Oscar's diction as if words alone could cure infertility.

A few scribbled notes like disciples copying scripture.

After the standing ovation, Oscar strutted toward me. "How'd I do?"

I patted his back. "You are the messiah."

Praise be to our door-busting, sweat-soaked savant.

We left the hall in search of breakfast. Oscar—fresh off inhaling a banana—tossed the peel onto the pavement like yesterday's data set.

A store clerk in a doorway watched the whole thing and gave him a look.

Suddenly, a parrot dive-bombed from a nearby perch. At first, it wasn't clear—was the bird after the banana peel, or after Oscar? It kept veering toward him, drawn maybe to that streak of white in his hair, mistaking it for plumage, a rival, or a mate.

Oscar panicked and lurched backward—straight onto the peel he'd dropped seconds earlier. We'd barely taken a few steps; it was still behind his heel.

Down he went.
Six-foot-six of genius—taken out by fruit and feathers.

Watching him slip, I saw the whole system in miniature: genius, ego, exhaustion, fruit on the floor.

He sat up, staggered to his feet, and blinked at me. "What the hell was that?"

The clerk shook his head and muttered, "Pardon the parrots and their banana peels."

We turned back. The parrot was happily shredding the peel to bits.

We both lost it—laughing hard enough to forget the sting of the morning. What else would you expect from an up-and-coming medical prophet? Every oracle starts somewhere, usually in a way that looks ridiculous in hindsight.

Breakfast never happened. I skipped the lunch-and-learn and grabbed a burger by the pool instead. Sea turtles slid past in the surf while we drank Kona beer and pretended the world wasn't waiting back in the convention hall.

Two physician friends from Mexico joined us, and the Oscar myth took over the afternoon. Each retelling had us doubled over. I don't think I've ever laughed harder. It became one of those perfect days—the setting right, the people in sync, the story so absurd that you could've died happy.

Oscar staggered into the pool area around 2 p.m., carrying a plastic bag of Spam musubi—Spam and rice pressed together and wrapped in seaweed. I tried one. Yuck.

By sunset, Oscar was woozy and starting to look sick. I asked when his flight back to New York was. "Eight," he said. "Tomorrow night."

I told him to take it easy, though that meant missing the after-parties. Not that it mattered—we were too burnt and too boozed by then anyway.

The next morning I woke to a text from Oscar: *Shit!*

His flight wasn't at 8 p.m.
Of course, it was at 8 a.m.

He needed $350 and a prayer the airline still had a seat.
I sent both before he could ask.

Who else was going to save him?
After all—my parrot boy wasn't God.

He was just a doctor. Another kid trying to get past the gates.

Cocaine

Cocaine is a fight with light.

First, the light swallows you—rabid, radiant. It tells you this is the truth. Then, it leaves. And the room remembers everything you tried to forget.

You rummage through the fibers of your lies and regrets. They fray in your hands. Light hardens into a life you knew, now out of reach.

Next comes the percussion. It taps your heart like a war drum—boom, boom, boom—not a rhythm of life, but of punishment. The hide pulls to its limit. A rip would be a relief.

After that, a phantom drip of arsenic slides from the left nostril. You touch it. Nothing's there.

Pressure gathers behind your eyes. The right eye. The left eye. The wrong eye. All of them feel like paper clamped in a vice, waiting for something to be written. But there's nothing to write. Nothing to say. Until the next line is laid.

I didn't think about any of this that night.

We had decided on the Saint Vitus Bar. A leftover organ of what New York City used to be, back when it still had an underground. A single-story refuge of bodies and bass—shadow, sweat, and sound. Strata upon strata. It didn't just illuminate you; it scorched you blind.

That part of my life lived in the blur. I was in my mid-thirties, nearly a decade inside the city. Not too old for impulse. Too young for restraint. The rules didn't disappear. They softened. Habit felt less like principle and more like something begging to be broken.

For years, I had resisted the drug. Not out of virtue—out of control. I liked knowing where the edge was, even if I spent my life circling it. Resistance gave me shape. Until it didn't.

Suddenly, you're standing there. A line of cocaine stares back.
Saying yes feels dangerous. Saying no feels rehearsed.
The moment stops feeling moral. It just asks, *What's the difference?*

I did my first line that night with Sam. The sensation was a razor blade. Sharp, but not sharp enough to cut. Not yet.

I stepped outside to meet Rick. I needed a cigarette—a small recess before everything sped up again.

I asked, "Do you ever think we inherit traditions we barely believe in, kept alive by habit?"

Rick took a drag. Let it hang.

"That's why we drink," he said. "Why we smoke. Why we snort."

"Maybe," I said. "Some people go the other way. Hide behind family and God. Pretend it cancels out the past."

Rick shrugged. "And they get real certain about what everyone else is doing wrong."

I flicked ash. "Seems cowardly."

Rick muttered, "Joey boy, they're bored."

"Boredom," I said. "We're the only species arrogant enough to get high on it."

Rick lit another cigarette. "Cheaper than cocaine."

After that, I did pull-ups on the scaffolding outside the bar. Eight. My record was ten. Maybe if I hadn't been smoking at the same time, I could've done more.

I flipped the cigarette like a paper football. It twirled once, ash collapsing in on itself. The ember dimmed. A breeze caught what was left and sent it drifting. The streetlight followed it—just for a second—and that flash pulled my eyes toward a fire hydrant.

Then, I saw her. Black Barbie.

I walked up to her and said nothing. I just kissed her. She didn't look at all shocked.

That's what those places do. Certain corners of the city loosen the rules.

I stepped back from Black Barbie and said, "Hey, baby, you want to do some blow?"

She hopped off the fire hydrant and splashed through a puddle, soaking her white Converse—scuffed the way they get after too many subway rides.

Inside, I went straight to Sam. I motioned a sniff, like a cartoon animal scratching for crumbs.

He barely looked at me—just enough to flip me the white dust and say, "Don't fall in love."

The mini plastic bag held the night in a few grams. And I had my apartment key in my pocket—grease-slick, warm from my hand. That mattered.

Seconds later, Black Barbie and I were inside a men's bathroom stall.

The stall was neon green and black, humid with sweat and piss. I took a bump. That bump became a road—a long, glittering one, paved in hubris and sport. Rage disappeared.

Black Barbie stayed close. Another line was laid. We snorted like pirates sharing spoils. I wiped the key on my pants and shoved it back into my pocket, then slammed her against the stall wall and kissed her again—hard, fast, like we were trying to devour whatever it was we were really hungry for.

I unzipped her pants. Slipped my fingers inside.
She moaned quietly—not for me, but for the pageantry of it.

Just as I was ready to keep going, she stopped me.
Pulled my fingers to her mouth. Sucked them clean.
"I wanted to taste myself on you," Black Barbie said.

I reached down again. She held my wrist. Enough was enough.

We left the stall with our secrets. Rick and Sam were on the dance floor.

That's when Chelsea appeared—the girl I'd gone on a date with weeks earlier. Not random. I'd texted her the address before the night had taken off. Some lazy *'come to me, baby.'*

Before Black Barbie.

She arrived with friends, dolled up like they were heading to a college reunion in the Connecticut suburbs. Polite dresses with seashells, paisleys—silk bows in their hair.

The kind of women I could date.
Easily. Respectably.
Just never quite mine.

I said something sweet, or at least I thought it was. "Tie me up with that bow."

She recoiled—everything spinning like a kid's kaleidoscope. Her friends stared around the room like they must have thought, *This must be hell.*

And it was. And it was great.

"We're not into this," Chelsea said.

I shrugged. "Enjoy the vibe. Don't chase the aesthetic."

She squinted. "Do you even know what you're saying?"

I grinned. "You better believe it, baby."

She looked at me like I'd gone mental. I had.

She and her friends left.

I turned back to Black Barbie. We collided again. She didn't know what the fuck was happening. Neither did I. The floor suctioned to our feet, stale beer and gray smoke coiling around us. The beat kept us from thinking.

Around three, we left. I kissed Black Barbie goodbye—forever. We got in a cab and crossed the Manhattan Bridge. It glowed blue. I stuck my head out the window and let out a *yahoo* meant to shake the steel.

Sam yelled, "We are going to die, motherfuckers!"

We laughed—like death was just a joke.

Then, we got quiet.
What if we did die?

The bridge didn't care. It held steady the way it always had. The bulbs along the railing winked at us, one after another, like someone counting backward. Their light slid across the cab window, across my face, then away. Each one smaller than the last.

I remember thinking: *This is the last clear moment.*
The car moved forward, and everything I could see fell behind us.
The river went black. The sky went black. My thoughts went black.

By morning, so did the rest of me.

I woke up in my apartment, shoes still on, mouth tasting like pennies. My phone was on the floor beside the bed. One message waited: *Never speak to me again.*

I stared at it a long time, like it might rewrite itself.

I'd met her four months earlier. Vivian. Her real name. In my head, she was Vinyl Viv.

She played records. Real vinyl. She lowered the needle like she was afraid the music might bruise. Sometimes it was terrible—fuzzed-out '90s girl rock—but it felt sacred because she made it feel that way. I'd watch from the couch, shirt half off, thinking this was the quiet I'd been looking for.

Even after I messed things up, she left the door cracked open. A late-night text she sent while I was at Saint Vitus, already deep in the noise. Something about a song we'd shared.

An invitation disguised as nothing.

Instead of leaning in, I spiraled inside the blackout. I answered high, mean, reckless. Sent a rant at five in the morning—all fire and fatalism. Then, I called. Thirty minutes on the log. I don't remember what I said. She did.

Maybe that's why I chose cocaine.

I heard the toilet flush. A naked woman came around the corner of my bedroom. It was a coworker. A late stray text must have convinced her. She lived close by.

She lay next to me. We'd had sex. Not a new mistake—just the same hollowness again.

I started thinking afterwards. Then crying.

Still, I reached for her thighs. She noticed the wet under my eyelids.

"Oh, you're a fucking mess, eh?" she said, stopping me.

I tried again—her tits, this time. *Denied.*

"Stop it. You have to get to Philadelphia. The conference, remember?" she warned me.

I lay there, head pounding. Still horny. Not for her. For Viv.

"I really miss her," I said.

"Didn't we just screw?" she asked. Not cruel. Just factual.

She looked at me long enough to know it wasn't about sex.

Her hand found my shoulder. "Get it together."

She started helping me pack. Shirts folded wrong. A belt shoved into a side pocket.

Then the blood came.

Dripping from my nose—the left side. My snort side.

Red jam streamed down my palm and wrist until I stuffed a tissue up my nostril. It felt like getting punched without the bruise—something leaking out from inside my skull.

Bloodstains aren't revelation.
Just waste. Taboos gone quiet.

I looked at the bloody tissue in my hand and thought: *So this is what curiosity costs.*

We finished packing. I said goodbye and got in an Uber.

Penn Station hit me like a supernova—lights blinking in and out, people pushing for space. I didn't fight it. The swirl in my head dropped into my chest. My heart said: *Go. Keep going.*

Then came the uniforms.

Blue suits. Cops. Dogs pacing the platform. I wondered if they could smell it—the residue still moving through my body. I was sure they knew everything. They sniffed. They passed.

So, I grabbed a beer.
Why stop now?

The train came. I crept on. The lights in my head dimmed. As we cleared the tunnel, the world went dark again. I was out cold.

I woke hours late.

My head throbbed with the static of withdrawal, my chest fluttering like a dying moth against glass. I felt like I'd crumbled into a dusty bowl of forgotten cereal, the milk gone sour.

That's when I realized I was in Philadelphia.

I got to the hotel, turned off the lights, and lay there waiting for the storm in my head to pass. The drip in my nose said it wouldn't. I wasn't done paying yet.

My coworker called. I told her I couldn't go on like this—couldn't keep moving my body while my mind stayed somewhere else.

She said, "It'll be fine tomorrow."

I said, "My chest is going to explode."

She said, "Then press your hand to your heart and remember you made it to Philadelphia."

Somehow, that helped. Not peace. Just enough to sit still. I turned on the TV. I didn't see what was playing. Just light. Sound. Noise. I hoped, when I slept, that I'd wake back up.

Around 6 a.m., I did.

I went to the conference. And no one knew.

Days later, when I got back from Philadelphia, it was raining in New York.

Outside Penn Station, a woman stopped me for directions to the Russian Tea Room. She mispronounced it—said *Wrush-in.* I didn't correct her. I pointed the way, knowing she'd ask five more people before she got there.

Still, something about that exchange felt clean.

I didn't have an umbrella, so I moved by instinct—awnings, scaffolding, doorways. Little islands of shelter. I zig-zagged toward the subway until I saw it: a soggy pack of Marlboro Reds.

Did I check it? Of course.
One cig was left.

Up ahead, a guy stood outside a bodega smoking. I asked for a light.

"Hell of a day, huh?"

He looked at the rain, then back at me, polite in that New York way that says 'hurry up' while still holding you a flame.

"Easy come, easy go," he said.

I nodded. "Thanks for the light."
The rain took him back.

A few nights later, I saw cocaine again.
It didn't shine anymore.
Just something waiting in the dark.

A Christmas Crooner in Blue Suede Shoes

There's very little to do on Christmas Day in New York City when you're alone.

Last year, I went to my ex's sister's place and wore the uniform—some V-neck sweater, a collared shirt underneath. I bet her mom was making her signature green bean casserole.

I'd miss that tonight—but I'd survive.

This year, despite having more PTO than I knew what to do with, I'd decided to use the holiday lull to finish a book I'd been working on for what felt like forever. I hadn't spoken about it much—especially in the last six months. If I ever did, someone would say, "You know nobody reads anymore."

As if that settled something.

The comfort of never finishing had begun to bother me as I approached forty. In wilder years, my progress had flirted with the page—quick bursts, half-commitments. Momentum built, stalled, built again. I slipped. Lost my grip. Drank heavier. Fucked faster. And the days became years.

All that chasing collapsed into me being alone.

Solitude became less a failure than a necessity. A strategic retreat. Most people my age never reached that quiet admission. Not because they couldn't—but because they drifted elsewhere. They settled into convention and learned to defend it.

They called it noble.

The noise comes later, when the choice needs explaining.
I chose to avoid the noise.

It was just past noon on Christmas Day, and I needed a break.

A stroll through my corner of Astoria felt right. If the day held, I'd take the subway into Manhattan—get off near Central Park and walk. Fifth Avenue was alive this time of year, the storefronts dressed with flair.

They offered a parade of innuendo—commerce sprinkled across those glass cubes of wonder.

I liked Tiffany's windows the best—not for the design, no, just their turquoise blue. It reminded me of the Caribbean, the one place I'd always meant to escape to. The chance had come and gone, swallowed by winter.

I left my apartment and rummaged through snowdrifts caked with salt and dirt—mounds of potatoes, really. I mashed through them. Most bodegas were dark, except for Mickey's Market.

I bought a pack of Marlboro Reds. I seldom smoked them. I preferred American Spirits (the yellow kind), but against my better judgment, I couldn't resist a little holiday consumerism.

The red-and-white label reminded me of Santa.

I splurged on a Diet Dr. Pepper. My recent attempt at sobriety had turned me into a soda addict. For some reason, the tannins reminded me of the sting of Chilean wines—hot-wine territory—where fermentation bites back.

What can I say? I liked the feeling of a tongue on fire.

Outside, my cigarette burned red, orange, and soot. A private fireside. Mine alone. Ash curled down faster than I expected, taking the illusion of time with it.

Right there, the question returned. Was writing stubbornness dressed up as belief...or the only thing I hadn't quit yet? Lately, that doubt kept circling my book—the last thing in my life that didn't come with guarantees.

My fingers went numb as I turned onto Steinway Street. "Silver Bells" played overhead from speakers bolted to lampposts. I slipped on ice in front of Gino's Pizzeria. Closed today.

The city wouldn't spread sand until the next morning. For now, tar sparkled, hugging the pavement like tinsel. The slick pavement sharpened irritation into judgment—the kind that comes when you're cold, tired, and spent.

I glanced at the holiday-red Marlboro pack in my shirt pocket.
I was branded—how phony of me.

The cancer sticks promise what everything else does: diversion. A softer edge. A way out of making anything at all. A life that never asks you to prove a thing.

Samuel Beckett would call this absurd: continuing without proof. Or maybe he had us fooled—after all, *Waiting for Godot* is his play. A performance about waiting that still expects an audience to show up.

Maybe faith is no different.
It asks only one thing of us: for us to keep going.

Most people don't quit on their dreams outright. They lean on circumstance—the job, the family, the dog—as if responsibility arrived uninvited, as if choosing had nothing to do with it.

What unsettles me isn't that people settle. It's how easily they crown the settlement sacred—rebellion boxed up like an old Halloween costume they never wore.

Permission granted.
Bailed out.

The world knows this. It just looks away.

I flicked the cigarette away and headed down the subway steps.
The cold followed me in, making me less mighty.

I swiped through the turnstile and looked up.
The train was delayed. Twenty-three minutes.

It was then that I recognized him—the man at the end of the platform. Charlie Wilson, a sixty-something crooner who impersonates Sammy Davis Jr.

I'd heard him here before. Same platform. Same song.

Wilson was hip with a Venmo QR code and a PayPal handle stickered to a water jug. Years ago, I'm sure it had been a bucket, a can, or a hat—spare coins and loose bills rattling at his feet. The same currency had powered the rest of it—then and now. Red, green, and white mini lights blinked from his speaker, a production propped against a bench stained with gum.

Whatever power fed the speaker pulsed through him. The lights caught his face in quick flashes, carving years of devotion into it. Time had left its mark there. Not as spectacle, but as proof.

His rubber lips sagged, basset-like, and whatever empathy I'd built began to recede.

His eyes carried the look of a man still auditioning for a dream long lost. One that would never be found—or so it seemed.

"I'll tell you a story about a man. He'd sing for you," he murmured.

I knew Wilson's story—he'd told it to me once before.

"It was '86. I had a gig in Vegas. Harrah's piano bar. Davis Jr. came by, and someone told him I was the best. We harmonized for a moment. I never looked back."

His story was stuck in the rags. His black suit said it all—pinstriped in red. If his blue suede shoes were any bigger, he'd risk parody, but their sharp tips saved him. Everything else had bent to winter: the suit, the swagger, the pant legs soaked in sludge.

"Mr. Bojangles," he whispered.

A tune made famous by Sammy Davis Jr., the Rat Pack outlier—smaller, Black, half-blind, never quite allowed to belong among men who never had to explain themselves.

Wilson had a different problem: impersonation. He borrowed a voice already weighted with history. And yet, he was Mr. Bojangles—embodying the myth of making it, long after the industry had moved on.

I sensed a private despair in that choice—not borrowed, but his own. As if part of him believed devotion could stand on its own.

Between songs, I asked him, "Why are you singing out here on Christmas?"

"Might run into someone who'll give me my big break." He winked.

I slipped a five into his cloudy jug.
Wilson nodded and went back to singing.

The train came at last.
Four stops to Central Park.

As I turned, Wilson caught my eye and tapped the old photo of him and Davis Jr. that he'd duct-taped to his setup. A moment frozen at Harrah's—when his god had seen him as chosen, if only for a breath.

I thought about how one day Mr. Bojangles would die. How the song wouldn't. Someone else would have to stand where he stood and carry it forward—without seeing who, if anyone, was listening.

Waiting was the only way to know.

My Mom, the Porn Dealer

In the winter of 1997, *Titanic* was an international box office sensation.

Theaters across the globe were jammed with people waiting to watch the romance between Jack and Rose unfold aboard a sinking ship. Even in Lewiston, Maine, the line curled around Hoyts Cinema like a wool scarf in December.

For me, the movie wasn't just a love story.
It was a gateway into the world of sex.

The introduction came courtesy of my grandfather, Poppop.

A few days before New Year's, my cousin Jeff and I stood in line at Hoyts Cinema when Poppop tried to give us a warning he didn't quite know how to deliver.

"Boys," he said, "I saw this flick last weekend with your grandmother. Keep your eyes out for the scene where they talk about drawing French girls."

He chuckled, proud of his disclosure.

We soon knew what he meant.

Inside, the theater was packed. Jeff and I got pushed into the front row while Poppop ended up a few rows back. In retrospect, it was a gift. Before the lights dimmed, I glanced back. Poppop caught my eye, cupped his hands around his mouth, and hollered down the aisle, "Joe—the French girls!"

I was eleven—an age where embarrassment and curiosity collide.
A moment when something in the male psyche shifts.

Kate Winslet, playing Rose, appeared on screen in a forest-green robe, walking toward a chaise lounge. The camera cut to Leonardo DiCaprio as Jack, arranging his canvas, easel, and paints. Then, Kate's robe slipped off her shoulders. Nothing revealed yet—just the camera teasing what was coming. DiCaprio stared, jaw unhinged. The shot flipped back to her face.

She said, "Jack, can you draw me like one of your French girls?"

I thought, *Here it is. Eyes open.*

And as if my grandfather's warnings weren't enough, I heard him cough six rows behind me—loud, guttural, like a lighthouse foghorn.

The anticipation was unbearable.

Then, in an anatomical flash of brilliance, Kate Winslet's breast filled the screen.

I clamped my hands over my eyes. I was one of those adolescents trained to do this whenever an adult scene appeared on TV—a reflex drilled into me by my overprotective mother.

My cousin Jeff, on the other hand—two years younger than me, all of nine—stared straight ahead at the mega-screen. His precocious appetite exceeded mine. Kate's breasts lit his face like a campfire, the boy baptized in cinematic flesh.

My cousin and I left the theater giggling—already plotting how to see more.

With no Pornhub, no OnlyFans, no Twitter feeds—and iPhones still science fiction—options were limited. Like for most boys, our key source was horror films.

Unbeknownst to my mother, standard slashers always carried a side order of sex. The hot girl flashes some skin, climbs on a D-lister, and just as the moment crests, Jason Voorhees, Freddy Krueger, or Michael Myers arrives to split the scene in two.

Of course, you never see the actual act in horror flicks. Just shadows, carefully framed movement, a thrust implied but never shown. Those doses of suggestion prepare you for what might come—a strange apprenticeship toward the sexually explicit.

I remember one movie in particular that drifted far beyond what a PG-13 rating ever promised, slipping into something closer to soft-core parody. If you're curious—and a little sick—it's called *Head of the Family*. Even typing it now, the title feels absurdly dirty.

The premise? A giant human brain in a wheelchair controls the lives of everyone in his warped little world. I'm pretty sure he survives on some combination of electricity and IV drip.

What lingered wasn't the kills or the grotesque characters, but the sheer overload of flesh. Everything became flesh. Tits, asses, dicks, vaginas everywhere.

No actual intercourse—just all the equipment laid out in advance of its use.

One specific scene burned into my memory: a woman tied up, hands fastened to a metal beam overhead, wearing only a tattered rag of a shirt. In a flash, it was torn away, leaving her completely bare. When you're shown all the forbidden parts at once, it feels like a riddle—you don't solve it.

You just stare.

I rented *Head of the Family* at least five times—probably more.

Eventually, those finds dried up. Another route presented itself: scrambled adult movies.

This peculiar rite of passage—sad as it sounds now—was an adventure. Before streaming and on-demand everything, we had cable, and if you didn't subscribe to the premium channels, the picture came through scrambled.

Cinemax, the sister channel to HBO, was infamous.

It was always after midnight. The screen green or blue, zebra-striped with neon distortion—the scrambled signal of a channel you didn't pay for. On rare occasions, as if God knew a pre-pubescent boy needed a thrill, the picture would drift into a heated scene and suddenly unscramble.

A shape unmistakably human.
A curve.
A movement.

Then—just as quickly—the stripes came roaring back.

Still, all of this was only a glimpse of what sex might be—touchstones, previews of wonder. None of it could have prepared me for my first encounter with hardcore, triple-X porn.

That came in the spring of 1998. Sixth grade.
I was just home from school.

I knew something was wrong. My mother wasn't crying, but she was determined. She placed my stepfather's clothes into boxes while he stood watching. Divorce hung in the room before anyone said the word.

Within months, it was final.
We sold our house.
Moved into my grandfather's home in a neighboring town.

What you should know about Poppop is that, after years in the Air Force and a stint performing as a clown, he kept a closet full of oddities: juggling balls, card tricks, magic hats, fake rabbits. I was told the closet was hands-off. A no-go zone.

Privacy invites curiosity.
By early summer, I gave in to it.

I'd been playing basketball with my cousin Jeff, the same one who hadn't averted his eyes during *Titanic*. After a long one-on-one session, we broke for lunch—bagel bites and Code Red Mountain Dew. Terrible nutrition, but at our ages, we could've eaten tar and survived.

After the break, we went rummaging through Poppop's closet. Forbidden territory. We pulled out juggling scarves, trick gadgets, the usual kid stuff.

Then, I spotted three VHS tapes stacked on the top shelf.

Two were jet black with neat white labels—the kind Poppop always used. One read *Routines for the Professional Clown*. The other, *The Pastor in You: Connecting with Your Community.*

The remaining tape was different.

Wedged between the others was a neon-orange VHS, bright as a construction cone.

I reached up and squinted at the label.

No Man's Land

Jeff and I stared at the neon plastic.

"Should we see what this is?" I asked.

"Sure. I mean, I've never seen an orange tape before," Jeff said—with an innocence that, looking back, disappeared far too early.

Even now, my heart jumps when I think of that moment. It felt like fate—a spark about to ignite. Moments later, we'd understand the meaning behind the word *nasty.*

We slid the tape into the VCR. Right before I pressed play, I noticed something strange. The reel wasn't at the start. It was halfway through.

My finger hit the play button.

Then the screen flickered, buzzed...INTERCOURSE.

To call this sensual love would've been an insult. This was an all-out, raunchy, sweaty, 'destroy-me-baby' kind of sexual bonanza. Processing it was impossible.

What burned itself into my brain was a man's throbbing member disappearing and reappearing inside a woman who, for reasons beyond me, was still wearing tennis shoes. Bent into a pretzel yoga pose, she was propped on a green felt pool table.

Kate Winslet suddenly seemed like a prude by comparison.

I slammed the stop button, and we bolted upstairs to the kitchen. Neither of us knew what to say. So, we did the only sensible thing. We ate more bagel bites.

A few minutes passed.

Then, Jeff said, "I want to watch more."

I answered, "I think that's a bad idea."

Jeff pushed back from the table, ready to sprint downstairs, but I stopped him—some older-cousin instinct kicking in.

"We can't," I said. "We aren't supposed to see things like that."

He looked at me like I'd just insulted him.

"Fuck that," Jeff said. "I'm going to watch."

He did. He rushed to the basement, and the sounds of women getting pulverized rose up the stairs. Soon, I crept down. Jeff sat back in Pop-pop's recliner like he was watching a Ken Burns documentary on anatomy—the sleazy kind.

That's when the panic hit. How the hell were we going to cover our tracks?

Luckily, I had my inexplicable gift of memory—every detail, every step before I slid that orange tape into the VCR.

"Jeff, we gotta put it back," I said. "Rewind it to where it was."

"No one will check," Jeff said—always so casual about these things.

I hit rewind and watched the counter tick backward, trying to land it exactly where we'd found it.

When we spot-checked it, we'd gone too far—closer to the beginning. That mistake helped explain why it was titled *No Man's Land*. Full-on lesbian porn. Even I couldn't resist ten seconds.

"Okay—enough," I said.

"This is the best part," Jeff said.

He wasn't wrong.

We corrected it—fast-forwarding, rewinding again—until we landed on a spot that felt safe.

Tape ejected, we sprinted to Poppop's closet.

Then, we went out back and played basketball.

Miraculously, we never got caught. Or at least never confronted about it. And if I said we didn't sneak peeks after that, I'd be lying. We did—every time, rewinding to the same spot, the same way.

Stealth became our currency in the pursuit of neon sex.

It took more than a decade before I confessed the crime. When I did, I never imagined who the real supplier of my boyhood rite of passage had been.

It came out at a bonfire. Too many beers. Friends scattered around the fire. My mother and sisters there, too. Somehow, the conversation drifted—as it does—to sex.

I told the story of the orange VHS tape. How gross it was.

My mother took a sip, laughed, and said, "I got that for Poppop."

Rarely do you hear a daughter admit she bought porn for her father.

"Mom, what are you talking about?" I asked.

"Yes, I bought those with your sister's dad," she said, as casually as if she were picking up cheese at the deli.

"Wait—your ex-husband?"

"Yes. I was too ashamed to buy it myself, so he went in, bought the tape, and handed it to me." She laid out the operation like it was nothing more than a grocery run to the IGA.

Let's take a step back—because for nearly ten years, I'd believed a very different story.

In my mind, Poppop had bought the tape himself at Old Orchard Beach, a landmark beach town in Maine. To be fair, it was a believable theory. Aside from the pier, French fries, and Lisa's Pizza, the real draw is its flea market. Vendors sold everything: baseball cards, beach chairs, and novelty gags like fake dog shit and whoopee cushions.

If you could imagine it, someone was hawking it.

Including porn.
Correction. Discounted porn.

Even as a kid, I knew the deal—one VHS for five bucks, or three for ten. There was no "back room" like at a video store. These guys were efficient. Cardboard boxes everywhere, each lid scrawled with categories in black marker:

Girl on Girl

Threesome

Regular

Back at the fire, I laid my theory out for my mother.

"So, why didn't he buy it himself?" I asked.

She said, "Poppop was too prideful. Too religious. He didn't want to look sketchy."

"So, he asked his daughter?"

"Yes. Why not?"

My mother and Poppop were close. Growing up, I'd never heard them change the subject when I entered the room. Whatever they were talking about—sex, money, God—it kept going.

Even so, my mother had moral boundaries. She couldn't bring herself to hand over "dirty money" to a guy selling smut. Which is how my mother's second ex-husband entered the picture.

Darrel was, at heart, a good man. His environment wasn't exactly pure. His friends weren't thugs, but they weren't saints, either. They were more likely to down a six-pack and chain-smoke than run five miles and drink protein shakes.

Still somehow on good terms, my mother asked her ex-husband to help buy porn for her father.

She picked him up around ten on some random Wednesday morning.

"He was a perfect accomplice—he knew where to find porn in our dingy mill town," she chuckled. "Better yet, he was willing to pay for it."

He told her to drive to a gas station downtown. Sitting in the car, he asked, "What kind does he like?"

In a family like ours, where nothing was off-limits, you'd think that question would've been settled already. But apparently this was one detail nobody had covered.

My mother didn't know what kind of porn to buy her father.
So, she consulted another family member.

That's where my grandmother enters the story.

According to my mother, my grandmother didn't hesitate. "Your father likes girls-only ones."

That suddenly made the title *No Man's Land* feel less ironic. Still, I don't know how—or why—men showed up in that piece of erotica.

Maybe bloopers?

My mother dropped Darrel off. The orange VHS tape, double-bagged in plastic, sat on the passenger seat. My mother later described the drive as "the most fearful time of my life." She was alone in her registered car, transporting lesbian porn meant for her father.

The possibilities spiraled.

Imagine a car accident. The tape would be found. Questions would follow. She'd be remembered as a loving mother, a devoted daughter—and a closeted lesbian.

So, she drove carefully, back roads only. All the way to her mother's apartment.

Now, remember—we lived with my grandfather. Why would my mother take the porn to my grandmother's place instead?

At the time, my grandmother was in the middle of a personal renaissance. After nearly forty years of marriage, she was newly single—fresh from divorcing Poppop. Not acrimonious. But she'd sworn off men entirely.

"Dumb men!" Her words. Not mine.

With separation came a kind of liberation. My grandmother began questioning not only her choices, but her identity—wondering who she really was.

For a brief moment, she even wondered if she might be a lesbian.

That temptation made her the final proofreader of my mother's bizarre mission. Before my mother handed the tape to my grandfather, my grandmother insisted on reviewing it.

"She said she knew what was good out there," my mother told us later.

Apparently, my grandmother had become the Siskel and Ebert of lesbian porn—with an intuitive sense of what would turn on her former husband.

For *No Man's Land*, she gave two thumbs-up.

Once approved, the tape was delivered.
My mother's role as porn mule was complete.

Around the fire that night, laughing and rolling our eyes at this deep, dark family secret, one question remained.

Where is the orange VHS tape?

Our days in Maine were long over. By now, my mother lived in Connecticut.

I leaned over. "So, where is the porn tape now?"

"In Maine," she said. "With Darrel."

Apparently, once she'd crossed state lines, her ex reclaimed what was technically his.

He'd been the buyer, after all.

Better Safe Than Sorry

I'd been drinking since eight. Not happy hour—8:00 a.m.
By noon, I was gunning for a personal best.

I stood near the ferry landing at the Battery, killing time in the sun. Three mimosas in, I turned to the Hudson for reassurance. Early June, sunshine bouncing off the surface. The ripples I usually spotted were smooth, as if my booze-soaked astigmatism had done the ironing. I squinted for turbulence. *Nothing.*

The river had never seemed so calm.

Ahead of me waited a brigade of willing fools bound for a champagne event in New Jersey, dressed in pastel armor—pink, yellow, blue, purple—beneath sagging yellow sponsor banners. Giant "V"s and "C"s flapped from every flagpole.

The Veuve Clicquot Polo Match is less sport than stunt—a champagne pilgrimage where men on horseback swing mallets at a small white ball while the crowd chases opulence, or at least its Instagram version.

For now, I was a party of one among the early swiggers. The morning kept getting uglier.

Two girls in pink and mint-green derby hats, dresses dyed to match, slouched on a curb in Battery Park as we waited for the ferry. One hand gripped a limp bottle of champagne, the other a bacon-egg-and-cheese bagel.

One said, *"Wow, have we really been drinking since seven a.m.?"*

The other: *"Drink it, babes—we can't drink on the ferry."*

That's the catch. No alcohol allowed on the field. Bags checked at entry.

The art of event-alcohol-smuggling peaked before the ferry arrived. I watched as others jammed nips into purses, tucked them into suit jackets, and even slid them down their socks.

Child's play compared to my covert operation.

The night before, I'd slit the bottom of a Triscuit box and carved room for a flask of gin beside the cracked-pepper squares. Bag stapled, box reglued, it looked wholesome again.

By morning, the crowd tightened at the final bag checkpoint. Paranoia stopped caring about craftsmanship.

Somewhere along the way, my flask rotated, pressing into the cardboard and warping the crackers' shape. A bulge swelled from the center. I tried to pat it down, crushing squares into crumbs. It didn't help. The "T" in Triscuit still had morning wood.

I stuck to a credo: when the cure promises more trouble than the disease, let it be. Biscuit boner or not, I carried on and prayed it passed for normal.

Then came Michelle, the bag checker, mere steps from the ferry landing. I knew her name because I always read name tags, offering that small recognition as if it might soften a scowl.

"You're good," she said, brushing me past without even looking.

I was almost disappointed. No pat-down, no suspicion.

She eased me toward the boats with her eyes. Mercy disguised as efficiency.

As I walked the plank toward the ferry, I fell in beside Cindy and her gay best friend, Jake.

Jake was a striking Asian American—the kind of man who, in my drunk imagination, could've been perfectly cast as Superman if the Man of Steel had come from Japan.

Cindy carried herself differently—composed, deliberate, dressed like someone who'd planned the day and paid for it. Her jeweled magenta mini-hat proclaimed: *Yes, I'm no longer in my twenties. No, I did not pick my outfit from Zara.*

I'd keep that judgment to myself.

We arrived at Liberty State Park and drifted together toward the polo field. Booze-fueled allies for the afternoon, we claimed a patch of lawn, the sun warming my face.

Suddenly unsettled, Jake sprang to life. "Let's get a bottle!" he declared, as if we'd perish without bubbly grape juice.

"I'm down," Cindy said calmly. "We've got a long day ahead of us."

Jake darted toward what looked like a fireworks stand. Every few minutes, a cork launched skyward, the crowd cheering as champagne frothed over them.

I stayed quiet, seeing only dollar signs. My secret stash was more than enough for today—and tomorrow. But who's counting?

Cindy glanced at me, then at the Triscuits.

"You're going to need something to wash those down." She grinned. "Is that all you brought?"

"No..." I hesitated. Should I expose what I had—or keep playing it cool?

Sitting beside Cindy, I felt the difference immediately. The sovereignty of a woman who knew what she wanted—and took it. Yet, here I was playing grown-up, hiding gin in Triscuit boxes. I was embarrassed. Ashamed.

Then, Cindy leaned in, smiling. "What kind of booze did you sneak in?" She tapped the box. "I used to smuggle flasks in potato chip bags. Worked every time."

I was stunned—and grateful.

She sweetened the deal. Reaching into a small cooler, she pulled out hummus.

"Good thing you brought the crisps," she said.

I thought I might be in love—and it was only 10 a.m.

Before I could process my emotions, Jake returned with a bottle and three flutes.

"This one's on me." He hoisted the bottle of Veuve like a golden trident. "Let's take turns. Joe, you got next?" He grinned as if we'd just sealed a sacred pact.

Cindy knew I wasn't quite established—or solvent—enough to drop a Benjamin on a single bottle. At twenty-six, in my first summer in the city, that kind of splurge still stung.

"He's got us covered in other ways," she said smoothly. "I've got next."

She winked at me while letting Jake know I'd brought the real drinks of the day. Jake's eyes widened, the allure of today's excess already outweighing tomorrow's hangover.

The rest of the day lost its outlines. I'm shouting, "Polo—polo—watch those horsies go, go!" I'm socially obliterated. Cindy and I get more handsy, stares turning into silent questions, silent questions into full-blown making out. Her magenta hat starts to collapse, pins loosening until it dangles unevenly, tapping her shoulders each time our necks adjust in sloppy, summer lust.

Meanwhile, Jake meets someone, and they slide instantly into intimacy—hands in back pockets, bodies close, standing nose to nose. Their approach is quieter, tender even, in the kind of romance that matches the pastoral façade: thoroughbreds on the field, blue sky overhead, champagne misting the air.

I'm too gone to care. Then, someone taps my shoulder.

"Dude, you're feeling pretty good. And it's only 1:00 p.m."

A Cheshire-cat smirk greets me—it's Brian, my college friend. He's finally made it.

Brian could've been God, and I would've greeted him the same way.

"Duuuuddddeeeee—yeeesssss!" I shout, hugging him and looking like an idiot.

Brian is more gracious. "Yes, I'm here." He grins. "Dude, I'm feeling pretty good. Drank before getting here, but I need to get on your level. Did you bring the gin?"

My head tilts, already euphoric.

"Where is it?" he asks.

I glance at Cindy's blanket: Triscuit dust, empty flutes, drained flasks—all consumed.

"Sorry, you should've come earlier," Cindy says.

"Oh, man. Well...whatever." Brian shrugs.

He rallies, pulling four miniature bottles from his jacket like contraband relics: Smirnoff, Ketel One, Jack Daniels, Captain Morgan. The caps crack like bacon as he downs two in quick succession, tossing Jack and the Captain into the growing graveyard of empties.

"Here, man—these two are for you. Can't stand the taste."

He hands me the vodka nips. I hold them like artifacts pried from a lost tomb in the Sahara.

This is the point of no return.

The point where I should hand the vodka to anyone else, drink water, and choose survival. But no—toe to toe with Brian, I crack the caps, swig the forbidden grain, and know instantly that my ticket is booked. All aboard the express line to Blackout Land.

After that, there's just *spots.*

My last memories are stitched to food. Pizza—Cindy next to me—the green polo field somehow morphing into a cobblestone avenue, taxis honking for preppy girls in pastel. Then, a Mexican torta—best when bought from a sweating man in a rickety food truck who slips in extra cheese because he knows how badly you need it.

And then...nothing.

I wake to the clatter of dishes. I'm not in my place. A quick survey. Diploma from Cornell, shelves of fashion books, a bottle of Burberry perfume. Waspy. I decide I'm okay with it. The apartment is tiny—a Murphy bed confirming it's barely big enough for one body, let alone two.

I turn, hoping it's Cindy at the sink. For a second, I grin, as if things are cool between us. But she doesn't return the expression.

"Cindy," I yawn.

"You need to go." Curt, flat. A sentence that lets me know I said or did something wrong. Or maybe she just feels guilty we hooked up. Then again, I wasn't sure we actually had. I start to ask, but stop myself. No use prying when I've already overstayed my welcome.

I get up, scrambling for my clothes. Cindy stays at the sink, scrubbing grease with militant focus.

"You okay?" I ask, more for me than her.

No answer.

I take one last look at her as I open the door, hoping she'll say something. Anything. A "goodbye" would suffice. Instead, silence.

My last image: *PINK*, in bold print down the leg of her Victoria's Secret sweatpants.

The morning is kind to me. I love the walk home in New York. The streets are quiet, stripped down, and in their desolation, you see how magnificent the city really is.

Inside Grand Central, I look up to the galaxy painted on the ceiling. At first, the stars dance like ballerinas, each pirouette measured. Then, the hammering in my skull ruins it—the stars turn break-dancers, dizzying and unbearable.

I need to get home. *Now.*

I dart to the 7 line—and, mercifully, it's waiting. I collapse into a seat, smiling in spite of myself, knowing I belong here. These are the moments when the city watches me, even when it knows I've misbehaved.

Before dying into my bed, I take a quick shower.
I don't feel much yet—everything's still dulled, delayed.

As the shower warms, I glance at the mirror to assess the damage. My face is tomato-red, baked by the sun. I step out. The air hits me, cold and clean. My skin rises in goosebumps, arms and legs stippled like a basketball's grip.

I catch my reflection again: scruff. I should shave, but I'm too tired. Still, work looms tomorrow. Shaving now means I can sleep in later. The thought of a longer morning in bed convinces me. I drag the razor across my face—a small sacrifice for my future self.

I forget to brush my teeth.
I collapse and sleep sixteen hours straight.

When I wake, it's to horror.

Is that a scab on my chin? I tap it while staring in the mirror. At first, it looks like dried toothpaste. *That's all it is*, I think. Residual paste sliding down my mouth from last night.

But then I remember—I never brushed my teeth.

My forefinger and middle finger circle the blemish. A small, enigmatic scab. I tap. Tap again.

I think: *Weird little zit on my chin.*
I hope: *No big deal. I'll pop it. Gone by tomorrow.*
I panic: *It's not popping!*

My body floods with cortisol and dread. My skin shines. I feel feverish. Sweat breaks across my brow. I tell myself: *It's just a scab. Just a scab.*

I start picking. Slowly at first, tracing the edges like peeling the sticker off a peach, hoping to lift it clean in one piece. If I do, I tell myself, it means it's healed—a neat discard of tissue.

But I'm not so lucky. Blood wells. I should stop, but I don't. With one swipe, I tear it off, like sliding a credit card at checkout. Better to bleed than let some glacial scab hang unchecked.

What I don't realize—what I refuse to consider—is that this thing was never just a scab. It had been brewing underneath the skin, contained and waiting. Once exposed, it's wasting no time.

Within minutes, a new crust asserts itself—not a clean seal, but a sticky, uneven bloom. Something ancient is coming back to haunt me, pushing up through the dermis. Yellow-brown ridges harden as they rise, stalactites forming from the inner cave of my chin.

This is the point where sane people would mutter about an infection. But not me. I'm a proud, practically impervious man. I cannot be subject to such weakness. Diseases are for unhealthy people, and I am not one of them.

So, my fingers lunge again, tearing away the mistake from the membrane. *Okay*, I reassure myself, *it's gone. Whatever it was—a little blood?—it'll dry out.*

Getting dressed for work is its own trial. I'm still nauseous from the cocktail of gin, vodka, and champagne—but worse is the unease of not knowing whether I had sex with Cindy. I must have. Why else would she have hidden herself away and told me to leave so abruptly?

As I pull on my shirt, my hand grazes my chin. The scab.

I rush to the mirror.

I think: *Holy shit.*

It's bigger than ever—no longer a single wound, but something active. The surface looks wet, glazed, as if it hasn't decided whether to seal or spread.

And it has spread. Not just throbbing on my chin—it's crept outward. Small lesions, sticky and pale at the edges, have bloomed along the line of my bottom lip, close enough to touch.

My head goes: *Fuck. Fuck. Fuck.*

I press at them—not bumps, not pimples, more like tender patches pretending to be skin.

Keeping cool in desperation is one thing. Keeping cool with a "growth" that looks like the ice goatee of the Winter Warlock from *Santa Claus is Comin' to Town* is another.

This was getting serious.
I needed to reevaluate.
Put one foot in front of the other.

Of course, the mind goes straight to the worst diagnosis. For any man, an unusual growth leads to one conclusion.

A sexually transmitted infection.

The internal STI conundrum unspooled in the same four-question order every man has asked since 1960.

Question 1: Did I hook up with that girl last night? — *Damn...I think so.*

Question 2: Shit. If I did, was I an idiot? Or did I wear a condom? — *For sure, an idiot.*

Then comes the true-or-false pee quiz.

Question 3: Does this hurt? — *A little? No...no, it doesn't. Or does it?*

I mull it over while scratching myself in useless solidarity. My genitals become a second me, disappointed with the weekend, questioning our character. So, I scratch harder. We're in this together.

Then, the final question arrives.

Question 4: Are my balls itching more than usual? — *No. Wait...kind of?*

Most people call their physician. I refuse.

Instead, I do what I always do when something feels unmanageable—I move.

I have work. A medical writing job at an infertility clinic, of all places.

Head down, I ride the N train to Midtown East.

I avoid eye contact.

Any blemish on your face feels like a public broadcast, something strangers can't help but notice. I hate myself for knowing that—for being one of the people who stare. I've done it countless times—a red zit on a pretty girl's nose, a lump on some guy's neck.

Now, I fear the same reaction. That as I walk up Madison Avenue, a small child might scream, *"Mommy, what's on his face? Mommy, I don't like it."*

Hey, kid, I don't like it either.

The elevator isn't transport today. It's a vanity trap, a steel box of imminent humiliation. I hesitate at the door. What if a coworker gets in and notices? I can't.

I step inside, hand hovering over my chin as a decoy. Quick survey. No one I know. Relief floods me. Then—*slam*. The doors open again. My chest tightens. My hand rises to cover my face.

Take cover.

But it's nobody. Just a stranger. The car lurches upward. I watch the numbers: fourth floor...sixth...eighth.

Almost there. Just make it to the tenth.

The elevator stops—ninth floor.

The doors open. *A mistake*, I tell myself. *Someone hit the wrong button.*

My CEO steps in, fiddling with his tape recorder. Fresh from a procedure, he doesn't look up. He just begins dictating.

"Patient had immediate bleeding after transfer. Catheter was full of mucus. Transfer was attempted twice to ensure all embryos were removed from catheter."

The panel of floor numbers doubles as a mirror, splitting our reflections into pieces. It's the only way we can see each other without looking. I stare at ten, fuzzing out the rest. Not enough. I catch him glancing at me. Briefly, but enough.

I pull out my phone—the universal decoy. I think: *I'm busy. I'm important. I belong here.* I pray for an email, a text, anything. Nothing. So, I scroll the inbox I already know by heart.

At the tenth floor, the doors slide open. I hold them for Dr. Gibson. He gives a half-wave.

"Have a good one, Joe."

My reply collapses into a stutter. "You, ta-ta too."

And just like that, the day tilts toward torment.

I walk to my desk like an angry drunk, brushing off morning greetings like dust. I don't have time for pleasantries. I need to hide.

Julio, of course, makes hiding impossible.

He talks to patients with the flair of a gigolo—the Spanish Casanova of the office. Officially, he's an infertility physician from Mexico City on sabbatical. Unofficially, he spends weekends marinating in tequila, salsa dancing, and forgetting it all by morning. He's also the closest thing I have to a best friend—and my chief confidant in all matters of sexual reproduction.

He hangs up after soothing a patient through the bad news: another $60,000 gone. Still no pregnancy. Only Julio could make someone feel okay about spending that much and getting nothing in return.

Then, he spots me. "Allll-right, here he is! Mi amigo!"

"Hey." My response is flat, distant.

"Hey, my friend—you okay?"

I point to Mount Rushmore on my chin. "See my souvenir."

"Dude, I don't see anything."

I want to punch him. His kindness isn't cute.

"Come on, man." I lean closer, forcing him to look.

He peers in, finally serious. "Umm...so, dude, I think I know what that is. Did you hook up with anyone this weekend?"

"Yes."

"Dude," Julio says, as carefully as one can in such a predicament, "I think it's herpes."

Panic rattles like a hundred jumping beans in a can.

I word-vomit. "What the fuck? I—what? How do I get rid of it?"

"It's okay. It's okay, dude. Relax. It's not as bad as it seems."

Julio studies me, eyebrows arched. Something in me turns feral.

"How can I relax?" I snap. "You don't have to deal with this!"

Julio bends toward me. "Dude, I have herpes, too. Hooked up with this girl five years ago—before I was married. Within days, my lips broke out. Same thing on my face."

"Sorry, man." And I am. "So, what happens next? Medication, therapy, quit my job?"

Julio chuckles. "Do you have any sores on your—you know—junk?"

I shake my head.

"Okay, then maybe it's not genital. Could just be Herpes Simplex. Less severe." He cups his crotch for emphasis.

I'm confused. Genital or Simplex? Do I even want the answer?

"Wait—so do you have..." I gesture over my lap.

"Oh—no, no, no." He waves his hands like it's radioactive. "The girl had a cold sore. After I kissed her, my face blew up. My dick is good." He shrugs.

We laugh. We needed it.

"Just get a blood test," he says. "That'll tell you. They'll probably give you cream for your chin, too."

"Fine. I'll get a blood test." I say it, surrendering.

You'd think someone in my office could help. But no. Rules, liability, optics—there's a line.

So, instead of walking down the hall, I call a local clinic like everyone else.

"Name? Insurance carrier?" the receptionist drones. "Reason for visit?"

"Blood work," I say. "And...a quick check-up."

"Yes, but blood work for what? I need to know what lab to send it to."

"STDs." I cringe.

"Which ones?"

I think: *Seriously? Do I have to order off the menu?*
I swallow, then say, "I'll get tested for everything. All of it."

But just as I'm ready to book the time, she asks, "For the check-up—what do you mean?"

I deflate. "There's a growth on my chin. It's...crusted over."

"Got it. How about 10:30?"

Her clipped tone tells me I sound worse than most. I confirm the appointment, hang up, and look at Julio.

"I've gotta go now," I say. "I'm gonna walk."

He nods once. No advice. No jokes. That somehow makes it worse.

I bolt.

The clinic feels dead—puke-green walls, pleather chairs squeaking in a symphony of shame. Then, a nurse appears at the end of the hallway. *Okay. This is it.*

"Joseph Lee." She stares right at me. I'm the only one in the waiting room.

I stand, legs rubbery, and follow her down a narrow hallway that smells like disinfectant and old coffee. Doors blur past. Somewhere behind one of them, someone coughs. Somewhere else, a printer whirs.

We stop. She gestures me inside a room.

She leaves, and I don't even know her name. Not that I'd remember it. I just want some human connection. Something. Anything. I miss life before this. Hell, I miss the waiting room chair.

I sit straight-backed on the crunching parchment paper, then give up and lie flat. Heat rises.

My eyes drift to the clipboard she's left behind—orders, not actions. In blue ink: *Blood Work. All STI. Growth on Chin/Lip. Crystallized. Possible Infection.*

A minute later, the door opens again. A nurse practitioner this time. No small talk.

"Arm," she says.

I offer it like a confession. The tourniquet snaps tight, rubber biting into skin. I look away as the needle goes in—a sharp, clean pinch, then the slow, obscene calm of blood filling the vial. One tube. Then another.

She presses gauze into the crook of my elbow and tapes it down. "Hold that."

I nod, suddenly aware of how quiet the room is.

"Okay, let me look at your chin." The nurse snaps on fresh gloves and prods. She scrapes a fleck of the crystal, then slides it under a microscope. The silence eats me alive.

"Is it herpes simplex?" I blurt. "Please, please say no."

She peers closer. "No. It's not. *Sorry*—just impetigo."

I screech, "Is that worse than herpes?"

She lets the silence stretch. Long enough to toy with me.

I press: "Um...is impetigo that bad?"

She peels off her gloves, tosses them away.

"It's a bacterial infection. Pretty common this time of year. A lot of guys get it in early summer. Probably nicked yourself shaving. Touched a subway railing."

She grabs a pen. "I'll write you a prescription for some antibacterial cream. It'll clear up in a day or two."

I say, "I thought it was herpes. My friend—he's a doctor—told me it might be."

She grimaces, points at my chin. "No. Your friend is wrong. You probably didn't need a blood test. Better safe than sorry. You'll get results in two weeks. Just call the office."

She slips out, leaving me on the crinkled parchment with a prescription in my hand. To her, it's just another Monday. To me, it's salvation.

I pay the receptionist on my way out. Thirty bucks. Co-pay. The cheapest relief I'll ever buy.

Within a week, the growth is gone.
Within two, the STI panel comes back negative.
All clear. Nothing contagious.

Then, a month later, Cindy texts: *Want to grab a drink?*

I refuse at first. She's become a symbol now—fear, assumption, pleather chairs, and one brash diagnosis. Still, I have to know.

Did we hook up?

So, I send the perviest text of my life: *Hey...after the polo match, did we have sex?*

The three dots appear. Hang. Mock me. Then—*bing.*

She texts: *No. You passed out at my place. I kicked you out.*

Turns out, the mystery infection was just me, inventing disasters like hobbies.

Lucky Me

You have the right to know this wasn't my fault.

Who among us hasn't been boxed in by six police vehicles on a Friday night? The story sounds worse than it was.

Let's start earlier that evening. I'm twenty-three. It's 2010. Boston. My keys are stuck in my apartment door.

I'd just come home from work—another miserable day as a research technician at Harvard Medical School, slicing two hundred zebrafish tails into tiny vials for genetic sequencing. Service to an esoteric gene no human would ever see.

Still, it was the start of the weekend. The night was just getting warmed up.

Oh, right—the key situation.

The key stuck in the lock. It had always been stubborn, but tonight the blue film on the cylinder told me the super had been there, undoing my muscle memory. I worked the old angles. Nothing. I tried again—less lift, more pressure. Finally, the lock gave.

When I pulled the key free, the copper was black—slick with oil.
My hands dripped with the lock's cold sweat.

My roommate Blake was on the couch watching his childhood favorite, *Camp Nowhere*—an unsung hero of Disney's '90s-kids-outsmart-the-adults era.

"Hey, what's the deal with the lock?" I asked.

He barely looked up. "Oh, Danny came by and replaced the panel around it."

"Look at all this grease," I muttered, black drips spotting my pant leg.

Blake laughed. "Give it a few days."

I needed a shower, so I soaked the keys in the sink before we went out.

Getting ready meant making myself look fresh to def—or at least, that's what I called it back then. Blake took hours, primping and adjusting until every detail was in place. When he finally emerged, it was always the same uniform: dark-wash jeans and a Ralph Lauren plaid button-up.

He spun once in the doorway, arms out. "So. Fab?"

I looked him over. "Aggressively."

He smiled, satisfied.

My night had a purpose—a reunion with an old flame. Samantha and I had never dated, but in college, we'd been late-night, drunken kissing buddies, the kind who blurred friendship into something else when Bon Jovi came on.

I hadn't seen her in a year, and I'd just broken up with my girlfriend. It felt like we were circling that same awkward space between friends and something else.

So, I dressed accordingly. More adult. More sartorial—or at least, that was the aim. My monthly subscription to *Gentleman's Quarterly* magazine—*GQ*, for short—had taught me that fit mattered more than flash. Somewhere in those glossy pages, I'd decided I was a French Canadian turning Italian, if only for the night—rebellious enough in Boston, an Irish town that still treated fashion like a suggestion.

I wore a lavender, long-sleeve V-neck from French Connection—an effeminate shirt I figured Samantha would appreciate. My favorite jeans were Lucky Brand indigos, the kind with *Lucky You* stitched inside the fly.

I imagined the moment: Samantha back at my place, the zipper undone, the hidden message revealed—humorous, or so I hoped.

A quick spritz of Blake's cologne finished the prep. We were ready—or so we thought.

Now, the keys came back into play.

I locked up to leave. When I pulled the key free, it was slick all over—fresh oil, darker than before. I couldn't risk ruining my Lucky Brand jeans with that sludge.

I went back inside and tried wiping the keys with a paper towel, but the shine stayed. I grabbed a plastic baggie—one meant for chopped carrots, not keys—locked up again, sealed the keys inside, and tucked them in my pocket.

Blake scoffed as we walked downstairs. "Ha—sure looks suspect."

"Why?"

He raised his hands. "Plastic bags. Weed. Cops looking for a reason."

Back in the early 2010s—before dispensaries and legalization—a baggie of anything looked incriminating. I knew it and shrugged. "True. But we're not going crazy tonight. Just hanging with Samantha. Maybe bringing her back here."

Blake cocked his head, grinning. "Oh really? My little Joey chasing Samantha's skirt?"

I winked, and he softened into the camaraderie.
Blake agreed to drive. It wasn't supposed to be a boozy night.

Samantha picked the place—a tourist trap near the South Seaport, not far from Quincy Market. The gimmick was simple: rudeness on purpose. At *Dick's Last Resort*, the hostess treated our arrival like an inconvenience, and the waiter called us imbeciles and dropped crayons on the table.

We ordered beers and skipped food. The place crawled with families—kids gnawing chicken fingers, parents pretending this counted as fun. Everything was red and yellow, the walls smeared with ketchup and mustard.

Blake and I were two drinks in. He'd caved and put on a paper hat, persuaded by a young waiter whose warm smile he mistook for interest.

"Where is she, man?" I asked. Samantha was an hour late.

"There she is." Blake pointed with his beer, face flushed.

Samantha always stood out in a quiet way—tall, nearly my height, with a slender, effortless frame and hair the color of sun-faded maple leaves, more amber than red. She looked like a '70s actress who'd never bothered aging into the '80s—slightly undone, just out of step.

I stood, trying to hold the cool Italian look I'd assembled. Samantha walked over in a short purple dress. I went in for a kiss, but she turned at the last second.

My lips grazed her cheek. Small thing. Still—a flinch in the script.

She laughed it off. "Look at Blakey! That hat fits you perfectly."

Blake said theatrically, "'Tis my pleasure to receive such applause."

Then, he kissed her hand.

I tried the same decorum, but Samantha pulled her hand away before I could reach it.

"So, my lady, why were you so late tonight?" Blake asked, no filter.

"Oh, I was with Josh," she said. "His coworkers were having a happy hour."

Blake smirked, squinting—not drunk, just theatrical.

"Josh?" he asked. "A new guy in your life?"

Samantha didn't hesitate. She sat a little straighter—the posture of someone who'd already decided on her man. "Yes. I met him a few months ago. He's great."

"That's great," Blake said. "Hopefully, we can meet him."

Samantha glanced at me. I'd seen that look before—another old flame going cold.

"Well," she said, a little bashful, "he's actually on his way. I hope that's okay?"

I nodded, still casual. Inside, my mind jumped ahead. I pictured Josh before I met him—solid, dependable. The kind who showed up. I could already see their life: Patriots Sundays, kids, a forward-moving certainty I'd always resisted. Simple. Sure. Beautiful in its way.

A flicker of jealousy hit me—not for Josh exactly, but for the life already decided. I masked it with a crooked smile and noticed a faint lipstick stain on her bottom left tooth—too subtle to mention, impossible not to see.

"Can't wait to meet him," I said, forcing ease into my tone.

Samantha looked relieved. She had every right.

Like most early post-college reunions, the night slipped into nostalgia.

"Remember that Halloween party?" Blake asked. "Joe lifted you, and you fell right on top of me."

Samantha laughed. "My back hurt for a week after that."

That was the rhythm—remembering nights when responsibility didn't matter, when we felt legitimate just because everyone else was there.

Then, Josh arrived.

"I'll go get him," Samantha said, already standing. She wove through the tables toward the entrance.

"This is going to suck balls," I muttered.

"Joey," Blake said, leaning in, "don't talk dirty to me."

Josh was nice. We shook hands and traded pleasantries. Nothing to grab onto. What do you say to the guy sleeping with a woman you've half-wanted for years?

It wasn't hostility. It was overlap.

Blake caught my eye—it was time. Samantha nodded when we said we had other plans. A former version of her might've tagged along. This one didn't. I noticed the difference.

We hugged. I gave her a look meant to say *I wish you well.*

We spilled onto the street, the night finally opening up. I thought about how easily doors closed—how Samantha had chosen something solid. Something finished.

And I realized, maybe too late, that I didn't want *finished* yet.

I wanted to stay open. Unclaimed. Alive.

I decided to risk it. Hell—what did I have to lose?

"Where to?" Blake asked.

"Gypsy," I said.

Gypsy—a perfect name. The most exclusive club in the city, just a block away. Its logo was an Egyptian lamp, smoke curling upward like a promise you weren't supposed to touch.

Blake grinned. "Think Jasmine is in there?"

"Only if you're the Genie," I said.

He snapped his fingers. "Baby, I've been waiting to come out."

I said, "You know there are six girls in there dancing inside glass orbs—lounging on silk pillows with pet tigers."

Blake laughed. "You're crazy, Joe. There's no way we're getting in."

He was right. Gypsy was nearly impossible unless you knew someone, were gorgeous, or had five hundred bucks for bottle service—which got you sad vodka and juice from concentrate.

Still, we stood in line anyway.

"We're getting in tonight," I said.

"How?" Blake asked.

I didn't have a plan. Or rather, the *plan* was to sound like someone who did. I cut the line, dragging Blake with me, and declared at the door, "Bottle service. Grey Goose."

I'd never seen a 300-pound man in an all-black suit light up so fast. Goose is a dumb bird. Put a four-figure tag on it, and people kneel.

Blake yanked my arm. "What the fuck, man? We can't afford it."

The bouncer raised a finger—signaling us to wait. He tapped his earpiece, murmuring, as if someone important might emerge.

Blake's eyes watered. My gut tightened. I wanted in—but at what cost?

A woman stepped out from behind the rope, clipboard tucked under her arm.

"Hi, I'm Rachel. You're interested in the Grey Goose service?"

She was spectacular. Everyone before her looked like an amateur.

Blake didn't wait. "Yes, we're interested."

She led us down a dim hallway washed in gold and plum. Persian rugs swallowed our steps.

The VIP section hovered over the floor—couches behind velvet ropes, power on display. Rachel guided us to an empty couch at the edge of a packed section—tables buzzing, bottles glowing.

Blake's euphoria faded. Mine, too. This wasn't the time to disappear. We'd come this far. Now, we had to get clever.

And then I saw him.

Through the smoke, an older guy was planted at the center of a booth, flanked by a mixed crowd—men pressed close, women settled in, drinks already circulating. Everyone angled toward him. The unspoken center of gravity.

I leaned toward Rachel. "That's my friend up there—let me say hi real quick."

She eyed me. "What's his name?"

I didn't slow down.

I hugged him and called him Uncle Charlie. Why Charlie? No idea. It just felt right. He was the bachelor-uncle archetype, still raging in his forties. I shoved Blake into him. Blake, quick on the uptake, embraced him, too—even kissed his cheek. Family reunion complete.

Rachel hovered, skeptical. But what could she do? We belonged.

She flashed him two fingers—not an order yet, just a question. Were these two with him?

For three seconds—the night froze. It felt like ten minutes.
Blake's half-smile said the jig was up.
Rachel pursed her lips, annoyed.

And Uncle Charlie?

His intoxication sharpened into clarity. Was he about to drop two grand on Grey Goose for two random dudes—or leave us humiliated on the sidewalk?

I gave him one last desperate look. *Just once. Hook us up.*
He nodded toward Rachel. The order stood.

I gave a dumb thumbs-up—like the end of a cheesy movie where the kid hits a home run and his dad tears up in silent pride.

Uncle Charlie had just hit a Grey Goose home run. Babe *fucking* Ruth.

"Bathroom," Charlie said, tapping his nose as he disappeared with some girls.

The rest of the booth held Red Sox execs—upper-level guys. One in ticketing, one in outreach. I asked who Charlie was.

"Some wealthy motherfucker," one said. "Bought a pile of Sox tickets and invited us out. We think he owns a modeling agency or something."

The night rolled on. Rachel delivered one of the Grey Goose bottles herself, a sparkler jammed in the spout, a little parade of glam trailing behind her.

She smirked. "Enjoy the night, you lucky son of a bitch."

We drank like kings.

To top it off, Gypsy was hosting a spectacle that night: *Search for Miss Boston*. A beauty-pageant warm-up for nationals—spray tans and sashes included.

Blake squinted at the stage. "Is that Jarod from *The Real World*?"

Before Instagram made everyone famous, MTV made a handful legendary. *The Real World* turned regular twenty-somethings into minor myths. Jarod was one of them, the clean-cut country boy cast in San Diego who made that reality-TV stardom look aspirational.

"Yeah," I said. "That's him. He must be hosting tonight."

Blake lit up. "Let's meet him. I want to say hi."

"Sure," I said. "Let's do it."

During a break in the contest, Jarod and his girlfriend drifted offstage onto the main floor, soaking up attention like it came with the job. Blake and I descended from the lofted VIP section and went straight for them.

Jarod was a full-time DJ. His girlfriend, Brittany, was a biology student at Tufts. Since I worked in medical research, I handed her my card. "My cell's on the back."

For a second, it felt cinematic—until Jarod sensed the shift. Maybe he thought I was trying to steal his girl. Maybe I was. He moved fast. His hand found the small of her back, automatic and possessive. He turned her away like a display being rotated, nodded once, and said, "Be well."

Then, they were gone. No opening. No sequel.

Rachel appeared beside us, all business now. "Charlie left," she said. "So, you're done here."

No accusation. No drama. Just math.

We threaded back through the club, past the rope that had felt ceremonial an hour earlier. Outside, the spell broke. We found the car—surprisingly quickly.

"Okay to drive?" I asked.

"I'm fine," Blake said with the confidence that only comes after too many drinks.

The night breeze slapped my eyes awake as we pulled onto Commonwealth Ave. I rested against the window, black air blowing kisses as we sped through it.

"I don't know how to get back," Blake said, casually, like it wasn't a problem.

"Keep it going," I said, blinking hard, elation hanging heavy. "Great night. Champions."

This was before your phone quietly saved you—before every wrong turn came with a calm blue arrow telling you where to go. No GPS glowing on the dash, either.

I called my ex from Quincy. She'd know the roads.

"Always at two a.m.," she sighed. "What do you want?"

I slurred something sad, nothing to do with directions.

"Where are you?" she asked.

"In a car with Blake—I love Blake."

"This is pointless," she said, and hung up on me.

Blake looped the same road again and again, making illegal U-turns like clockwork. Then, finally, he veered left. The city changed fast around us.

Gypsy silk gave way to Brockton asphalt—low brick buildings, flickering streetlights, liquor stores with barred windows. A street that doesn't ask what you're doing there. Just watches to see how long you last.

By then, we were operating on a dangerous assumption—that if the night had let us through this much, it would keep doing so. Little did we know that was about to change.

Up ahead, a haggard man drifted along the curb, hood half-zipped, hands buried deep in his pockets, pacing like he was waiting for someone. Or something.

Blake honked. "Hey—you walking there. Which way back to Brighton?"

The man turned toward us. Came closer. And then—*everything*. Six Brockton police cars lit up the street and boxed us in. It happened fast.

Blake was pulled out first—hands up, voice soft, apologizing for something.

I was half-turned in my seat when I heard the yelling: "Put your hands up! Put them up!"

I hesitated with the phone in my hand.

A cell phone and a gun aren't the same thing—but under paranoia, both pass for a concealed weapon. The cop barked, "Fucking idiot! Put your hands up, asshole!"

I shoved the phone into my Lucky Brand pocket. Hands up.

The passenger door burst open. A cop hurled me to the ground, nearly ripping my collar off. Face to the tar, cheek grinding in gravel, I did the one thing you should never do in that position. I laughed.

"What's so funny, dick?"

"Officer, we're innocent. We—are—good—boys."

"Yeah," he said. "You look like some good boys."

"Where are the drugs?" another voice shouted.

Suddenly, a knee drove into my back, my shoulders torqued tight.

"What's in the pockets?" an officer demanded.

He pulled everything out.

Being searched is a bizarre intimacy—like someone reading your diary, only worse: public, humiliating, smelling like lint.

First came my crappy Verizon flip phone—my last starter phone before the iPhone. Then my wallet. A thick block stuffed with expired credit cards, insurance slips, junk I no longer needed. Tucked inside—the real relic—an old Abercrombie & Fitch employee card.

Back then, Abercrombie wasn't just a store. It was a hierarchy—cologne clouds, shirtless greeters, kids pretending to be chosen. I kept the card. Laminated proof of a status that no longer applied.

My elements of Ivy didn't even register. The cop flicked it aside.

Then, he reached my right pocket. The crinkle of the baggie was death in my ears.

"What the fuck is this?" The officer's knee drove deeper into my back.

My head scraped the pavement. Pebbles lined my cheekbone like sand at the beach—except I couldn't wipe this off.

"My keys," I said.

"Why are they in a plastic bag? Huh? Were there drugs in here? Where are the drugs?"

"Greasy keys," I said, surprised to hear myself smile at how absurd it sounded.

"What the fuck are you talking about?"

"I didn't want my pants to get greasy. Our lock was changed. The keys were covered in oil."

"Greasy keys?" He paused. "Have you been drinking?"

Some questions are so dumb that they don't deserve answers. They still get them.

"Yeah, officer," I slurred.

He pointed at Blake. "Has he been drinking?"

"Yes. Of course," I said.

Blake's tears dried into rage. He glared at me like I'd just ratted him out in a plea bargain.

Still thinking we were on the same team, I chirped, "How about you fellas?"

The cops didn't laugh. They got louder—voices sharper, movements more aggressive—as if volume could manufacture certainty. In their minds, this was the bust.

Then came the curveball.

"Hey. I'm the drug dealer you're looking for."
The guy we'd beeped at earlier said it flatly. Almost bored.

Everything shifted. The knee lifted off my back. The cuffs came off. The cops pivoted with brutal efficiency and slammed the real dealer into a brick wall, cuffing him like it had been the plan all along.

"You two, go home. Right now!" one officer snapped. It landed hollow. His authority had sprung a leak.

"Why were you even in this area?" another asked.

"We're lost," Blake said. "Trying to get back to Brighton."

"Next time, ask the police," he said, pointing past the flashing lights—straight at the Brockton Police Station, mere steps away.

The drive back was silent.
It deserved to be.

We entered the apartment feeling like we'd pulled off the greatest drug heist in Boston history. Maybe I wanted to hold onto the high—or maybe I just liked watching power trip over itself. Either way, I had the urge to call the Brockton Police Department and give them a piece of my mind.

I dialed. Straight to voicemail. I said:

Hello, my name is Joseph Lee. Tonight, I was falsely accused of dealing drugs by officers of the Brockton Police Department and thrown to the ground before they realized their mistake. I am a good citizen. I work in medical research. I pay taxes. I demand better training, better conduct, better accountability. How am I supposed to trust a city that treats people like criminals for asking directions? You can reach me at josephadamlee87@gmail.com

I hung up feeling righteous.

The next day was recovery. A scratch under my eye stung just enough to be noticed. My back ached like I'd swum miles. Even reaching for a cereal bowl felt like work.

Then—*bing*. An email from an unfamiliar address:

Mr. Lee,

We have received your email regarding the incident earlier this morning – Saturday, July 24, 2010. If you would like to speak further, you may come to the station and we can discuss.

Yours truly,
Sergeant Crawford
Brockton Police Department

Did I want to go to the police station? No.

I replied:

Dear Sergeant,

I'm happy the real perpetrator is in custody. Thank you for your kind email.

Joe

Not an admission of guilt. Just an omission of embarrassment.

I wasn't wanted.
I was spared.

Lucky me.

The Jesus Parade

My earliest memories of religion take me back to the lowlife.

It's 1989. I'm three years old. Drunks, smokers, and prostitutes nod along to a fuzzy Johnny Cash gospel special on a cube-shaped television. I'm perched on the jittery knee of a schizophrenic woman who believes she has aliens in her head.

Some of this, I remember the way a body remembers—through smoke, song, and vibration. Other parts came later—family stories retold, photographs passed around, VHS tapes digitized.

So, let's rewind.

My grandparents—Meme and Poppop—decided to become Ambassadors for Christ, starting what would now look like a cult for the couponed and condemned. You know the type. People with flea-market reflexes, always on the hunt for a deal, with shabby pasts known but unspoken.

The gospel refuge was called the Coffee House, tucked into Lewiston, Maine. Perched in the dead center of the city's former skid row, Lisbon Street, our headquarters sat wedged between pawn shops, flophouses, and busted neon signs that hadn't blinked right since the '70s.

Legend said the place used to be a butcher shop for horse meat—racehorses, specifically. A house of horror became a house of holy by nothing more than a lease agreement and first month's rent. Maybe that was fitting. Meme had a soft spot for the worn-out thoroughbreds of Lewiston.

With no soup kitchen, shelter, or government handout in sight, the Coffee House drew the town's marked souls—the kind of people whose names made others cross the street or, if they were brave enough, step inside for a cup of burnt coffee. Outsiders glanced through the window and decided whatever they needed to decide in one breath. Inside, there were no rankings. No one needed Jesus more than anyone else. You could pray, sit quietly, or just take what was given. Some days, salvation came disguised as day-old donuts.

The donuts deserved their own gospel. Not because they were free, but because they were ritual. Al, the owner at Labadie's Bakery over on Lincoln Street, had a gentleman's agreement with Meme. He'd leave a bag of rejects on the side of the dumpster each night—on the condition she picked them up. "Otherwise," he'd say, "the raccoons'll tear 'em to bits."

So, it became a nightly errand for my mother and me.

We'd pull into the lot behind Labadie's, where a trash bag leaned out of a tank-like dumpster just far enough for a grab-and-go. She was the wheelwoman, I the cardinal of curbside. My job was to snatch the holy bag. On occasion, no bag leaned out—and I'd find myself dumpster-diving headfirst, elbow-deep in pastry purgatory, groping around for a sack of salvation.

The next morning, we'd head to the Coffee House. We sorted through the dumpster donuts, preserving the sweet grit of working-class faith. My mother started the coffee pots. I spread the day-olds out before the morning crowd shuffled in.

These weren't donuts. They were *offerings*.

Faith, as Meme lived it, wasn't symbolic. Her theology didn't ask you to surrender your friends, your joy, or your life. It wasn't followership; it was belief—a grab bag of Catholic, Christian, and Protestant tones. Confusing, maybe, but personal. Not punitive. As long as you treated people right and believed the debt was already paid, that was enough.

The gospel according to Meme rested on one simple scripture: *If you believed Jesus hung on the cross and died for your sins, salvation was granted—Paid in Full.*

She even screen-printed the slogan on teal T-shirts—cheap cotton with a black cross and a blocky sign stamped across the chest: PAID IN FULL. Meme handed them out like uniforms.

I still have one that fits.

Meme kept things lively around the Coffee House, putting that simple scripture to work. Along with Poppop, she'd host open-mic–style concerts. One Saturday night, during a raucous rendition of "The Blood-Bought Church," things really heated up. Cloth napkins were swung overhead, the room catching a fever as the singing spilled into something rowdy.

For a boy, this was glorious—the swirling sensation of assumed believers, arms linked and forming a conga line, looping through the cramped Coffee House, belting lyrics way beyond my years about blood, an army, praise, and swords—marching straight out of Revelation.

It must have been a warm August evening, because the weather whispered for us to go outside. Meme yelped, "Let's show the Lord what we really got!"

We did.

The group paraded around the block, past the convenience store, while smokers and lottery-ticket scratchers watched us float by. One even joined in, flapping his losing Mega Bucks ticket like the torn wing of a green neon angel—half saint, half sucker, looking for a second chance.

We circled Chestnut Street and slipped back through the Coffee House's rear entrance off Park Alley. Inside, we looked at each other in disbelief. We had broken code—we'd left our holy ground and taken to the pavement. And just when we thought the song was over, Poppop struck up another, and back out we went into the streets for what felt like an eternity.

It was the dumbest, most magical thing.
I never believed like that again.

Jesus, does anyone?

That was just one night in a place that made the ordinary feel sacred. There was always another scheme underway—less like a church revival, more like a sideshow for souls.

Nothing captured Meme's holy hustle better than her infamous fortune-telling routine.

Now, picture this. Meme wasn't some cloaked sorceress with a trembling veil. She was dressed in what can only be described as the '80s biggest fashion misstep—a bubblegum-pink denim jumpsuit, cinched tight with a studded belt, her perm haloing her head like she'd just stuck a fork in a toaster. Thick amber glasses completed the ensemble.

Right outside the Coffee House hung a sign—crudely scrawled in Sharpie, placed beside a crooked tarot card symbol: *GET YOUR FORTUNE TOLD...FREE.* And people came.

Meme would usher them past the linoleum tables, the cracked coffee urn, and the wire cage where her pet chinchillas—Mary and Moses—spun endlessly like fur-covered prophecies. Then, she'd guide them through the squeaky back door and into what had once been a coat closet, now transformed into her fortune-telling studio.

At the center of a tiny round table sat what looked like a crystal ball, draped in a white handkerchief. Meme would circle it slowly, murmuring vague promises about the path ahead and where a drifter might go in life—lines loose enough to mean everything and nothing at the same time.

Then came the hook: "Are you going to Heaven?"

Some laughed. Most hesitated. A look that said: *I'm not sure. How do you know?*

That's when she'd whip off the cloth, revealing not a crystal ball, but an upside-down carnival fishbowl. Under the glass, glued to the tabletop with dried Elmer's, sat a chocolate-brown cross, circled with chinchilla dust like cemetery dirt.

Straightening her glasses, she'd deliver the verdict with rehearsed certainty: "You'll go to Heaven if you believe *He Paid in Full.*"

She said it like a punchline, but it came from a bruise the church had given her.

I came to understand the Coffee House wasn't born of whim. It grew from disillusionment—an intentional step away from pulpits that no longer spoke for people like us.

You don't lose faith all at once. It frays. Americans watched the threads give way when televangelist Jimmy Swaggart—the TV preacher who cried on camera after getting caught paying for sex—fell from grace. Lewiston knew hypocrisy when it saw it. Surrounded by prostitutes who came through the Coffee House, I never thought them worse than Swaggart. At least they weren't selling holiness by the hour.

So, Meme built something smaller. No cameras. No polished apologies. Just people trying.

Among those holy misfits, one man stood out:
Henry Mustard Face—a scratchy man with a hot dog addiction.

If you've never been to Maine, here's something to know. Our hot dogs are red. Not pink. Not "kind of" red. Popsicle red. Bright, violent, stuffed with pig parts and whatever else the FDA hadn't gotten around to banning in the late '80s. Which made mustard impossible to miss—electric yellow slicing straight through crimson. Ketchup disappeared. Mustard testified.

Just down the street from the Coffee House sat Simone's Hot Dog Stand on Chestnut—one dollar for a dog and a Coke, a deal too good for Henry to ignore. Afterward, he'd wander over for donut dessert and air his daily grievances. He arrived like clockwork.

Meme would start. "Henry, you got mustard on your face."

Henry's lawnmower voice rasped back, "What? I do? Dang bun must've had a grenade in it."

"Henry, I've known you for ten years," Meme said, already smiling. "Every day...the same stubborn blob welded to your cheek like a postage stamp."

"Ah, come on, Margey!" He waved us off. "Don't give me a hard time. My check don't come in 'til tomorrow. Just give me a napkin. The Lord forgives—I repent—and all that jazz."

Then, Henry would turn to me. "Hey, kid—do I got mustard on my face?"

"Yes. Right there," I'd say, pointing.

He'd plop down at his usual table by the window facing Lisbon Street. "Pass the ashtray."

I'd bring it along with a fresh cup of coffee—early training for the service business. The mustard stayed put.

"Wipe it off!" Meme called, now half-annoyed.

"Hold your horses. I'm stirring the Cremora!" Henry barked back.

Cremora was the Coffee House's only luxury. Not milk. A chalky powder that lived somewhere between dairy and drywall. Every table had a tub.

Henry stirred—always three turns—then took a long gulp.

Meme handed him a napkin. "Use this."

"I don't need that," he said.

With careful ceremony, he dragged the rim of his Styrofoam cup along the mustard crease of his lip like a squeegee. Rotated the cup. Clean rim. Problem solved.

"See that, kid?" he asked, proud. "That was smart."

When left alone with his thoughts, Henry Mustard Face would pull a crumpled pack of cigarettes from his shirt pocket, pat it against the table, and light up. Speaking to no one in particular, he'd say, "Nice day today. Looks like everyone's having a good one. Y'know what? I'm having a good day, too."

That was Henry. A man who showed up, took what was given, and made a day out of it. Meme loved him the way you love a wayward son who keeps coming back, bruised but still trying. She never asked him to change. Just to sit. Drink his coffee. Laugh through the smear on his face.

And for a while, that was enough.

The Coffee House carried on—hosting concerts, dancing, and even a wedding—for another decade or so. Before it all came apart. Before Henry Mustard Face stopped showing up. Before the room emptied in ways you don't notice until it's too late.

But belief needs a stage. A grand finale.

There are only two kinds of endings: the proud send-off that lets you say, *It was a good run.* Or the kind that leaves a sour aftertaste—the one that makes you ask, *Why the hell did we start this in the first place?*

I'll let you guess which one the Coffee House got.

By then, I was about thirteen. We were buzzing in the days leading up to what would become family lore.

The Jesus Parade.

This wasn't a Coffee House production, but the Maine State Easter Parade. A sanctioned, civic affair. Big enough for sponsors. Big enough for God, as long as He didn't get too weird.

On the drive to the staging area, I sat in the back of my mother's Nissan Sentra—the only car I remember from adolescence. I was eating a chocolate cruller from Dunkin' Donuts, wedged between my cousin Rick and my two sisters, Sharon and Olivia. I'd just entered the age of acne. A hard blemish sat on my nose. Another on my chin.

My younger sister pointed at both, tapping them like buttons. "What are those dots?"

My mother snapped, "Olivia, don't touch!"

I asked, self-consciously, "What dots?"

Rick chimed in, "Those are zits. Duh. Act-me—or whatever it's called."

"Maahhh, I don't want to do this stupid parade," I groaned. "Everyone at school's gonna see."

My mother turned halfway in her seat, her voice calm but final: "Joe, this is really important to Meme. Okay?"

Right as she said that, we hit a speed bump. I'd just taken a bite of my cruller and accidentally bit the inside of my lip. It started to bleed.

Olivia: "Joe's bleeding, Mom! I can't tell if it's his *act-me* or if he bit his tongue."

Mother: "Olivia, stop it. Joe, what's going on?"

Sharon, dry as ever from the front seat, said, "His sacrifice for our sins."

We arrived at the float staging area, and it was immediately clear this wasn't some small-town mess. This parade had money. Floats with polish. Big, well-decorated trailers with frilled borders, vibrant paint jobs, and sound systems. Costumes. Choreography. A touch of Broadway meets county fair.

We were told we were in Section 4A.
As we pulled in, we saw our float.

An eight-by-twelve platform. Rusted metal framing. Warped, sun-bleached plywood.

Rick squinted. "Ours looks like a piece of crap."

My mother snapped, "Rick, be quiet! I don't want anyone saying anything negative about this float. Meme will be here soon."

Right on cue, Meme rolled up in her powder-blue Honda Civic, Poppop behind the wheel.

Poppop climbed out first, took one look at the float, and then leaned back toward Meme, who was still unbuckling herself from the passenger seat.

"Um, hey, Marge. Uh, this is bad."

Meme stepped onto the pavement, surveyed the sagging plywood and rusted frame, and beamed.

"Oh, stop it—this is great."

She popped open the Civic's trunk and pulled out a black trash bag—her version of sacred storage. Inside were cardboard cutouts. Only men, for some reason. Three feet tall. Flat. Painted like cartoon saints—robes, sandals, and exaggerated beards. Each had a hole punched through the top of its head.

At first, we didn't think much of it. The figures felt generic—vaguely biblical, racially ambiguous. In our optimism, we assumed this was Meme's attempt at inclusivity. God's love for all people.

Then, we saw the labels.
Not names—roles.

Painted in thick black letters across their chests.

Teacher
Policeman
Priest

Then, the next ones.

Murderer
Burglar
Pedophile

Yes. *Pedophile.*

Meme's idea was simple, if unhinged: We were fishing for sinners.

We tied line through the holes and hooked the cardboard men to fishing poles. Meme positioned empty plastic salt buckets upside-down in a rectangle on the float. We grandkids were expected to sit on them, poles in hand, with the cutouts dangling in midair—swaying, bobbing, suspended like human bait.

Before social services caught wind of the plan, the pushback had already arrived.

My mother, always accommodating, leaned toward Poppop. "Dad," she said quietly, "pedophile...that one's a little aggressive."

Poppop sighed. "Another one says *Rapist.*"

Yes. *Rapist.* Just when you thought the embarrassment couldn't get any worse.

At thirteen, I should've known what that meant. But growing up with a protective mother—one who'd banned *Looney Tunes* for violence and *The Simpsons* for being too raunchy—I honestly thought the label said *Rapper*.

Right then, Aunt Keri strolled in, XL Dunkin' in hand. "Sorry we're laaaate. Hi, everyone. So, this is the float?" She eyed it, then Meme. "Reaaal niiice, Mooom."

Her son Alex, seven years old, was told to sit beside Olivia. Meme handed him the *Rapist*.

Rick noticed and threw a fit. A budding hip-hop aficionado, he'd wanted to hold the *Rapper*.

"Maybe Alex can give it to Rick," Aunt Keri suggested.

"No!" Meme snapped. "That's Alex's."

Aunt Keri squinted. "Wait—why do you even have a *Rapper* on cardboard?"

"Rapper?" Meme waved her off. "What's a Rapper? Get moving, I don't have time for this. We've got twenty minutes until start time."

My mother was about to burst.

"Mom, what's so funny?" I asked.

"It doesn't say R-A-P-P-E-R!" she exploded. "It says R-A-P-I-S-T."

Poppop raised his hands. "Hey, calm down. You can't be yelling that. I'm the only man here."

Sharon, dry as ever: "Glory hallelujah."

Aunt Keri yanked the cardboard defiler from Alex's hands. "My son is not holding a 'Rapist' sign. This is ridiculous." She turned to Olivia. "Which one are you holding?"

Olivia glanced down. "A pedophile?"

"I'll take that one, too," Aunt Keri said, grabbing it.

A few Coffee House regulars drifted over, drawn by the commotion.

I leaned toward my older sister. "What's a rapist?"

"A bad thing," Sharon said.

"What's so bad?" I waited.

And that's when Henry—drool fresh as morning dew, lips hanging like forgotten laundry—looked up and said, "Somehow...aren't we all raped by God?"

As vile as that statement was—and it absolutely was—the moment passed. Meme and the parents had the good sense to move us along. No follow-ups. Just forward motion.

Poppop stepped in. "Joe," he said, "how about you and Rick push the tires?"

Yet another piece of parade paraphernalia. Two industrial black inner tubes for Rick and me to roll down the street. No longer were we on fishing pole duty. Each tire was painted in bold white letters.

One read:
GOD IS LOVE
JESUS = YES

The other:
JESUS SAVES
PAID IN FULL

It was almost time. The parade was lining up. Then, one last trick up Meme's sleeve.

From the trunk of the Civic, Meme pulled out her toolkit—deck screws, scraps of PVC pipe, a power drill. "Make a cross," she said, handing it all to my mother.

A craftswoman in her own right, my mother knew what to do.

"At the end of the parade," Meme added, "we'll zip-tie his hands to the piping. Joe and Rick will help."

So, who would be Jesus?

As you probably guessed, Henry volunteered. He always did.
He'd carry the cross on his right side—his mustard-face side.

Naturally, Meme produced a white garment—diaper-like—cut from a faded bedsheet. Henry changed between the open car doors of the Sentra. Shirt off. Belly out. Outie belly button like a badge. The only time I ever saw him shirtless.

There was a crown of thorns, too—twigs gathered from Meme's daily jaunts through Kennedy Park, a former drug-deal hotspot. Fortunately for Henry, she didn't press it into his scalp.

Henry yawned. "If only my mother could see me now. I was her prodigal son."

So, with G-rated sinners swinging from fishing poles, the rickety float lurched forward behind a loose tow from the Nissan Sentra. Henry Mustard Face walked in front of it all. Rick and I trailed behind him, rolling two giant rubber tires like disciples with no plan.

Just before we started moving, Meme chirped, gleeful: "Ambassadors for Christ—go, Jesus!"

Most of the route was dead. Desolate streets. Empty porches. A few confused neighbors waving from lawn chairs like they already regretted coming outside. It felt familiar—another quiet stretch of a dying town.

Then, we hit the last tenth of a mile.
Every parade has one. The gauntlet.

The place where everyone who knows you has lined the curb near the food trucks and souvenir stands, waiting for a spectacle.

Faces popped out of the crowd like whack-a-moles from Sunday school. Brian from math class. Ashley from social studies. I could feel their parents watching Henry Mustard Face—diaper, crown of twigs, the whole situation.

Kids whispered, "What is their float even about?"

Parents replied, arms crossed, "Don't worry about it."

Or, "I'm not sure."

Or, "Do you want cotton candy?"

Then, I saw Casey.

I hoped she wouldn't see me. That's how you know it was a crush—the kind you don't recognize until it's already doomed. Early love is just a feeling without a name. Maybe God sent me an angel. If so, He was also cock-blocking me. In His name.

I did what thirteen-year-olds do. Studied the pavement—the geometry of disappearance.

But no—she saw me.
We locked eyes. Briefly. Long enough.

The parade kept moving. The end was near.

We still had one last encore.

Every float ended at Main and Mill Street, just before the bridge to Auburn, where Lewiston and Auburn split at the Androscoggin River like ex-lovers still pretending to get along. This was the last spotlight—the place where local news crews, city council types, church officials, and overzealous uncles with VHS camcorders waited for a performance, where marching bands hit their loudest note and dance teams sold their brightest grin.

We didn't have brass.
We didn't have sequins.

We had Henry Mustard Face.

Just as we reached the curb, Meme shouted, "Boys! Hold up the cross!"

Rick and I dropped our tires. We ran and lifted the PVC cross Henry had been carrying and raised it upright. Meme climbed down from the float and approached him. From her pocket, she pulled out zip ties and fastened his wrists to each arm of the cross.

Henry didn't resist. Years in the Coffee House had trained him well. He knew not to break character. He tilted his head to the side, sorrow pooling in his eyes—solemn as a thrift-store saint.

Then, Meme reached into her battered L.L. Bean canvas tote and pulled out a tube of cheap red paint—the child-grade kind from aisle nine at Marden's discount store.

She squeezed a glob onto Henry's ribcage and smeared it with her fingers, like she was finger-painting *The Passion of The Christ*.

The crowd froze. No one knew what to do with what they were seeing. Was this devotion? Protest? A joke gone feral? Silence answered for everyone: This was not okay.

And in that very second, I had a thought I've never been able to unthink. *If we actually stabbed Henry in the rib, would mustard come out?*

But there he was—Henry Mustard Face. Crucified for our sins. Hanging on tippy toes, dripping with poster paint and pride. I knew, as you do now, he'd rise again tomorrow. Coke in one hand. Hot dog in the other. Like nothing had happened.

Then came the signal from the parade volunteer: "Okay, that's your time—move out."

We cut the zip ties and lowered the cross onto Henry's shoulder.
He was the Messiah. At least for the day.

Back home, we huddled around the television. Meme had taped the whole parade on VHS. We fast-forwarded, hunting for our moment—the little reward you hope for after public humiliation. But the news skipped right past us. The camera cut away.

Henry died off-screen.
Even that felt ceremonial.

My family worshipped the story of *The Jesus Parade* more than any page from the Bible. It became our accidental rite of passage—not a spelling bee win, not a first kiss behind the middle school, not even a Little League walk-off.

Our coming-of-age arrived through the strange absurdity of the Coffee House.

One night, a few weeks later, I asked my mother, quietly, "Do you think we really believed in all that Jesus stuff? Or were we just afraid not to?"

She didn't flinch.

"All faith, no matter its package, stems from fear," she said. Then, folding a sock, she added, "But we dressed it up as love. That's what makes it convincing."

In that moment, religion didn't feel foreign. Or scary. It felt like a neighborhood—run-down, weird-smelling, familiar. A place where comfort still lived. Where even a losing lottery ticket could be the right piece of flair for dancing in the streets.

And whether there's an afterlife or not, I've learned this: We won't know until we get there.

But some things you know now. A mother folding warm towels on the kitchen table. A raised eyebrow. A half-smirk—the brave, cavalier look families like ours pass down. A glance that says: *The whole world be damned. They're not like us. They never will be.*

My mother knew how to pass that along.
Like Meme, she was Paid in Full.

Sex Saved the Summer

You don't usually follow a one-night stand with a trip to the hardware store. But that's exactly what happened. Champagne, pull-ups, and a shattered sink.

The mishap was nearly a year in the making.

It started on November 11, 2017—the last time I had sex with my then girlfriend. A week later, I ended the relationship; it was the classic pre-holiday split, a mercy break before the *"Wanna meet my parents?"* question started to linger.

"At least we had a good summer," she said.

"Have a nice Thanksgiving," I said.

She puffed, "Whatever."

That's how things end when civility still matters.

But winter in New York turns that freedom into frostbite. From December through March, nobody wants to leave their apartment—let alone strip down and pretend to care about someone else's body heat. A blanket turned human burrito, a premium DoorDash account, and endless streaming become the survival kit for the weary kind.

In due time, desire turns practical.
It tells you to get laid—fast.

Rebound sex isn't therapy; it's triage. It's how you stitch your ego back together before you start Googling your ex or writing poems that begin with *"You are not my person."*

Honestly, you don't even care who you have sex with.

By March, I met Amber—smart, funny, into old films, and the kind of woman who'd pretend to understand your dream of writing the Great American Novel. An unexpected lifeline, courtesy of my friend Brian, who was trying to shack up with her roommate, Cindy.

We met at Brian's apartment in Chelsea—a crash pad so overused that I practically had my mail sent there. Things started slow. I wasn't on my game.

Wine and takeout Indian food helped loosen the nerves.

Somewhere between Amber talking about her dad's obsession with Jimmy Buffett and me overanalyzing "Cheeseburger in Paradise," a mutual sense of sensuality fried into being. Grease-slicked and wine-lipped, half-buzzed on fermented chicken tikka masala, we started making out on the couch. Right in front of Brian and Cindy.

Then, they made out, too.

It didn't last long—maybe it was the hush between smacking lips or the half-curious glances we kept sneaking at each other from the side. Or perhaps our little free-love festival sputtered out for a simpler reason. It was a Tuesday night, after all—a school night, in spirit—and work was waiting in the morning.

Amber pulled back. Her lipstick had lost all discipline—wine-stained, zigzagged, smudged like a toddler had gone rogue with a blackberry crayon. Her grin held that familiar gloss of bad decisions and cheap Côtes du Rhône.

Laughing through her breath, she turned to Cindy. "We should go."

Cindy nodded.

Amber looked back at me. "I'll text you later this week."

The girls scooped up their bags and headed out. The door clicked shut behind them.

Brian exhaled and slumped into his chair. "Well," he said, "that was wild."

"Sure was," I said, joining him at the café table.

Outside, the Joyce Theater hummed across Eighth Avenue, its low electric glow painting our faces in pink and blue. Between us, two empty glasses caught the neon like tiny crystal crimes.

Leaning out the apartment's window, I caught the girls climbing into a cab. I waved. They didn't see me. The taillights slid down the block—red starlight fading into black.

Not over the hump just yet, I thought. *Progress, not perfection.*

A few nights later, I was four whiskeys deep, midway through a YouTube rabbit hole titled "Top Ten Reasons You Shouldn't Be a Writer."

Reason #5—"Because no one cares about your trauma"—hit a little too close to home.

Then came a text from Amber: *Margarita night with the girls. Meet me afterwards?*

With the prospect of redemption buzzing in my pocket, I took another pull from the bottle and told myself I was preparing for greatness. I was Hemingway with Wi-Fi.

It was just before midnight when I met Amber at some East Village dive. Initial small talk circled around a novel idea I'd had that week. "It's going to be massive—something about death before relevance. It might save lives!" I said it loud and loose, tapping the table like a bar-band drummer on his last encore—less swagger, more bruised underside.

She nodded—amused, perhaps intrigued—then sliced through the bullshit.

"Want to go to my place?"

I didn't answer. We just left.

Outside the dive, I ducked into a bodega and grabbed two tallboys.

I cracked one open—paper-bag koozie in hand—as she led the way.

Somewhere between that beer and the bed, there was a blackout.

When I woke up, jeans still on, she was gone. The room smelled like an alley cat's paradise. Then came the wet realization. I'd pissed myself.

She was on the couch when I crept out.

"Hey, you...?" I began.

Silence. Then, flat as a dial tone: "Leave."

In a half-drunk haze, I botched my exit. "Mind if I grab the last beer from the fridge?"

"Sure," she said, shielding her face from the sun. "On your way to piss on someone else's bed?"

I took the beer. Fuck it.

Later that day, she sent a Venmo request: *Five hundred bucks for the damages.*

I paid it—happily. Sent a pathetic *sorry* text.

A few days later, I even bought her flowers and had them sent to her office in midtown.

Apparently a bad move.

Upon receiving them, she texted: *Had to explain to my coworkers who sent these.*

I wrote back: *Did you say my soon-to-be boyfriend, Joe Lee?*

Part of me thought humor might turn things around.

She wrote: *More like Pee Pee Lee.*

Ouch.

Then: *Don't pull any more stunts.*

I replied: *Sure. Can we talk this out?*

Immediately: *No...never again.*

Fair enough.

After a stone-cold rejection like that, I spent the next day pretending it didn't bother me. But humiliation has a way of hanging around—especially in a city where the smell of urine is as ubiquitous as your own decay.

The following night, over Greek food with Brian and his roommate Mac, they broke into hysterics until the table shook.

"Pee Pee Lee—classic," Mac said, tzatziki nearly shooting out of his nose.

All I could think was how one bathroom break could've changed everything—maybe Amber, maybe the slump, maybe the whole damn quest for a rebound.

When a drought drags on, time becomes its own mockery—weeks blur into months, and paranoia starts spinning like a black-and-white hypnosis wheel—faster, tighter, sucking you in. When the wheel stops, you start digging up bones—exes, hookups, half-remembered nights. You fire off "hey" texts like a gambler feeding quarters into a broken slot machine.

The phone buzzes, hope spikes, and then it's your mother asking how you are, a coworker wondering why you're late, or worse, a former fling delivering the mercy kill: *Delete my number.*

Sometimes, they add *asshole* for punctuation.

A drought is hard for a man because sex isn't just pleasure—it's proof.

If we're screwing, we're surviving.
Broke? Fine.
Hungover? Fine.

But involuntarily celibate—*whatever that means*? That's failure pretending to be nonchalant.

Two more months passed.
March swiftly became May.
Half a year, a new virgin.

So, what's one to do?

Naturally, I thought a change of scenery might succeed where therapy couldn't. New city, new luck.

Me, Mac, and Brian rolled the dice in Miami.

Conveniently, our friend Theo was living there on a six-month "investment stint"—one of those vague ventures that sound impressive until you realize it might be a Ponzi scheme.

His building was called *The Icon*.

The lobby lived up to the name—glittering chandeliers, lemon-water greetings, and marble floors that smelled like money. But inside his unit? The same old bachelor squalor: pizza boxes, a coffee table missing a leg, and blue painter's tape marking the future couch.

Luckily, there were four barstools.

Mac popped open a beer. "Boys, this weekend's about two things—sun and sin."

I raised mine. "To the hunt."

Brian grinned. "Not all of us are hunting, champ. Some of us are starving."

I squinted. "Didn't you snag Cindy?"

His grin dropped. "No!" He lurched forward, half-reaching for my throat. "After you pissed Amber's bed, she figured it was best if *we* kept some distance."

Didn't realize I'd cockblocked by consequence.

I cracked another beer. "We better get laid this weekend. But where? On these stools?"

"Hell, I'd fuck on the floor," he said.

Theo cackled. "Don't worry, boys—Amazon's coming with blow-up mattresses."

By evening, the concierge dropped off the boxes—no pump included. We blew them up mouth-to-spout, each breath a sad little prayer to the gods of temporary pleasure.

Somehow, Mac still had a little gas in the tank.

"Little surprise, gents." He lifted his phone like a preacher boy at first communion. "Cabana at Nikki Beach. Brunch on the Beach—babes, beats, bottles. Thongs soaked in vodka soda."

Brian grinned. "Dude, that's sick."

Theo shook his head. "You sly bastard, that's *the* spot."

Soon after, we called it a night and fell into our air beds.

By 11 a.m., we were at Nikki Beach. Prime location. A beach club with overpriced cushions and umbrellas, bottles of Cîroc for five hundred—mixers included—a sunlit temple to South Beach shenanigans.

For a few hours, we weren't four washed-up romantics. We were kings.

Mac linked up early with a bottle-service girl.
Theo had a girlfriend back in New York and wore it like a curse.
Brian and I approached a pair of Palm Beach divorcées.

Norma and Betty.

Norma had a son at Pepperdine in Los Angeles. "A future entrepreneur, a real go-getter," she said. "Building an app for mentorship—or mentorship for apps. Something like that."

Betty had entrepreneurial ambitions of her own—launching a Pop Rock lip-gloss line. "Your lips tingle all day long. Who doesn't like twenty-four-seven stimulation?"

Norma raised her glass. "Sign me up, babe!"

Cougars, if there ever were any.

That's when I drifted—a casualty of needing to take a leak and brushing past the other partygoers. On my way back from the bathroom, still steadying myself toward our cabana, someone shouted, "Hey, you! Get your ass over here!"

That's when I met Tom—a pint-sized tech bro from New Orleans.

He hooked me like a cowboy snagging a calf and pulled me straight into his barrel chest. "You son of a bitch, I like you. You got something."

"Maybe 'cause I'm French?"

"Hell yeah!" His teeth flashed in the Miami sun. "You one of those *je ne sais quoi* types."

He shoved a shot into my hand.

"To France," I said, then gulped.

After that, we took another.

Soon, all I remember is laughter, some yelling, and a wave crashing just before...blackout.

Again.

When I woke up in Theo's apartment, my phone was on the floor beside me—with a text from Brian: *You passed out at Nikki Beach. Took you back. We went out again.*

I patted my thighs. Dry—thank God.
I sat up, the tile cold beneath my feet.
Fresh air felt necessary.

Out on the balcony, the sea-salt air felt like a gentle hand rubbing my back. I lit a cigarette and let it all spool through me. Prevailing wisdom says a man in my position should just suck it up—but even city cowboys run out of road.

Sure, it's easy to dump girls, book trips, and run wild and free—but freedom curdles when it's just repetition in disguise. The warmth of a woman softens demons that refuse to die.

Miami had pulled my linchpin.

My energy was scorched to its last fuse. I'd started believing I was an afterthought. The kind of doubt that digs its heels into places you thought were hardened long ago. But self-pity had never suited me.

I needed proof that angels still walked among us.

I dialed my ex—the one from November—and laid it out.

"I guess it's been tough since we broke up."

"It's 2:30 a.m. Why are you calling me?"

I didn't say anything for a while. Maybe I was waiting for grace, or maybe I just wanted to hear her breathing on the other end. I liked to think she remembered us.

She let the silence stretch, then offered one word.

"Sorry."

I didn't reply. She hung up.

I almost wept. I caught it before the first tear formed, my lip trembling instead.

Then, the pain.

Back inside, the bathroom mirror confirmed it. Small blisters across my lips—angry, raw. Miami had left me a souvenir. The burn was brutal.

Unsure where the nearest pharmacy was—or just afraid of what else the night had left to teach me—I found some ice in the kitchen and pressed it to my mouth.

After ten minutes, I walked back to bed.

The next morning came with glory chants.

Mac had boinked the bottle-service girl.
Brian allegedly hooked up with Norma.
Theo ended up eating pizza with a guy who'd just gotten engaged.

"What about Betty?" I asked.

Brian gave me that look. "Done deal, until you passed out."

I touched my lips. "Also—what the hell happened here?"

"Must have been the Pop Rock lip gloss." He paused with curiosity. "You and Betty were making out hardcore in the ocean. Then you were gone for half an hour."

I rubbed my jaw. "I was ripping tequila shots with some tech bro."

Brian tilted his head. "Around sunset, you looked dead. So, we dumped you in an Uber."

Mac punched my shoulder. "Yeah, fucker, you puked in the backseat. My only one-star rating."

I rubbed my eyes, piecing it together.

"Damn," I said. "I could've had Betty?"

"No doubt." Brian's hands hovered over my crotch like he was blessing it. "MILF maaaagiiiic."

That evening, we flew back to New York. I slept the whole way.

The next morning, my lips were torn up. My desire had flatlined, still paying for the night before.

Time to figure out my shit.

The best remedy was discipline, or so I told myself.

So, I started running again, cut out cocaine, and even swapped tequila for turmeric. Tried reading before bed instead of doomscrolling. Told myself I wasn't chasing sex anymore.

Nothing else was working.

I kept it up for a few weeks. Even volunteered at a food shelter on Saturdays, handing out cans of corn like they were second chances. For a while, it felt good—holy, even. I'd become the patron saint of misplaced guilt. But virtue has a shelf life; do it too long, and it starts to smell like denial.

And like most in denial, I started online dating.

What a mistake.

Modern courtship felt less like romance and more like a job application—good deeds for credit, small talk for leverage. I kept swiping through the digital bazaar of maybes and almosts, each match feeling like a soft interview for intimacy.

I was chasing romance via spreadsheets.

My old rugged charm—and whatever outlaw scent I had left—was gone. I'd gone choir boy on the dating apps. No surprise, women saw right through me. Nothing dries up desire faster than someone trying to be polite about it.

Once, over dinner with a Puerto Rican girl, I actually asked, "May I kiss your lips ever so tenderly?"

What the fuck was that?

A stack of bad dates will teach you that lust isn't logical.

Then, one random morning in July, brushing my teeth, I caught my reflection—a moment where honesty cornered me. Through the toothpaste smears on the mirror, I saw the worst kind of disappointment: a man gone soft—not in body, but in conviction.

I'm not the first to stumble.
Not the first to bail on bravado.
Not the last to say, "I'm taking *time* for myself."

The bullshit we rebrand as strength.

Eventually impulse prevails, and the dam breaks.
Where sex turns chaos into order—if only for a moment.

August hit. It was time for some chaos.
One last summer bash sat on the calendar.

The evening was thick with humidity; I was already sticky. Mac, Brian, and I rolled up to one of those all-white parties—a pre-COVID phenomenon where everyone dressed head-to-toe in white linen and pretended it was glamorous.

We looked like angels, but behaved like devils.

Set in Brooklyn, naturally, the lawn in Prospect Park looked like a detergent commercial for a cult that mandated white shirts, pants, and dresses—a kind of Hamptons cosplay for the broke and ambitious. Bums drifted past pushing grocery-cart caravans through the trees, and the pond shimmered with syringe tips glinting like fallen constellations. Even the swans looked hooked on heroin, circling lazily for another fix of breadcrumbs and sanity.

By sunset, the sober looked smug, the drunk looked holy, and everyone pretended their loneliness was networking.

That's when we met them—three girls.

One had a boyfriend in the army. One took to Mac. Brian had brought his new girlfriend, Stacey. Which left me with the last girl in the group—silent, composed, and laser-focused. She scanned. All poise and precision, like a cyborg on standby.

To this day, I still don't know her name.

No matter. Somehow, I ended up making out with her.
No build-up. No slow burn.
Just spur of the moment.

Then came the after-party.

The seven of us crammed into a cab, a fever pitch of limbs and liquor. We darted to 170 Eighth Avenue—Club 170, as it became known. Not a bar, not a club—just Mac and Brian's cramped Chelsea apartment.

Where else would we go?

When we arrived, the place was primed for destruction—champagne bottles stacked like trophies, music pulsing through the drywall. On cue, I peeled off my shirt—maybe Freudian, perhaps just me—and started doing pull-ups from a doorway bar. Not scaffolding. Just a tension rod held up by IKEA witchcraft and Allen-wrench sorcery.

I hit ten—a personal best that summer.

The girl with no name watched. Silent. Still. Scanning me for weaknesses. Then, she leaned into Brian's ear and whispered something that sent him sprinting toward me.

"She says you're her dream man. Hottest guy she's ever seen."

"Damn right," I said—because what else do you say when you're drunk, shirtless, and halfway to believing your own myth?

And yet—even in my need for sex, I hesitated. Was it really this easy?

By midnight, people had started peeling off. The party was thinning. The soon-to-be army wife slipped out. Then, mystery moans drifted from behind closed doors.

The girl with no name and I made our way toward the kitchen. I thought we were leaving. But no—she had other plans. She backed me into the trash can and said, "Sit down."

Then, she unzipped my pants and went to work.

Suddenly, Stacey—Brian's new girlfriend—walked in. She froze at the sight of someone getting head, then scurried off like a cat who'd just witnessed something deeply human.

Even then, the girl with no name and I weren't done.

"Your place or mine?" I asked.

She smirked. "How about the bathroom? I love doing it on a sink."

Odd request. But after ten months without touch, I wasn't about to negotiate. Efficiency is its own aphrodisiac. She grabbed my hand and yanked me down the hall.

Tally ho, I thought, the door slamming behind us like a starting gun.

I stripped. She hiked.
A few thrusts—
One Mississippi,
two Mississippis,
three Mississippi—

and then...*CRASH.*

The sink cracked clean off the wall.
Porcelain exploded across brownstone tile.
Shrapnel from a war that never meant to sign a truce.

The dreamscape spun off its axis.

She grabbed her stuff and vanished.

Then came Mac—normally all smiles and swagger, but not tonight. He stormed into the doorway, eyes bugged, hair wild, voice cracking with betrayal.

"Get out! Or fix it! I don't care!"

I just stood there thinking:
At least it didn't break my foot.
At least water isn't spraying everywhere.
At least I got laid. Sort of.

Brian walked me downstairs like the good friend he was. We half-laughed, scheduled a plumber, and grabbed a slice of pepperoni pizza—a small victory lap after a long night of bad decisions.

After polishing off the crust, we returned to the apartment. I passed out on the couch.

The next morning, a van pulled up with a hand-painted logo—*Two Hearts Plumbing: We Fix What Life Breaks.* Out stepped a man in his fifties with a plumber's crack that could moonlight as a canyon. His wife sat in the passenger seat knitting. A true mom-and-pop operation—if Mom and Pop also slept in the van.

"You're the second sink this week," he said, peering into the bathroom.

Brian and I locked eyes—half disbelief, half spiritual awakening.

"Do you think...?" I said.

"Could it be—a pattern?" Brian added.

It wasn't far-fetched. People get off on all kinds of things—feet in Jell-O, feathers, latex, silly string. But the girl with no name? Maybe breaking sinks was her thing.

"Yeah, that's not up to code," the plumber muttered. "Landlord should have replaced this long ago."

I saw my out. "So...the landlord pays?"

He shined the flashlight at the destruction. "Sure. If you like waiting six months for hot water, too."

Mac had left earlier to run errands—a clear message he didn't want to be around for any of this. Even if he was squeezing avocados at Whole Foods, I could already hear his rage cracking the pit. So, I did what any guilt-ridden guest would do. I offered to pay.

"Tell you what," the plumber said. "Come to the hardware store. Pick the parts you wanna buy."

"Fine," I said.

On the drive, he talked the whole way—union wages, sink trends, his wife's gout. Then, halfway down 23rd Street, he glanced over.

"You'd be surprised how many people break sinks during sex."

I nodded. "Maybe she's a serial sink fucker."

He chuckled. "Kid, if she is, she's a legend."

At the hardware store, I picked the cheapest replacement I could find—plain white, no frills, built for endurance, not a romantic massacre.

"That model's gonna cost you two hundred an hour to install," he said.

"Two hundred?" I asked. "What are you, a lawyer?"

He wiped his hands on his jeans. "Lawyers bill you to stay clean. I charge to deal with your shit."

"So be it," I said. "I'll pay you whatever."

He grinned. "Okay—since you shared a good story, I'll do it for a hundred an hour."

Finally, a little compassion.

We returned to the scene of the crime. By noon, the sink was fixed.

The plumber shook my hand like we'd buried something sacred.

In a way, we had.

Then, I did what any man does after paying four hundred bucks to fix someone else's sink—I played tennis with Brian.

We took a break, wiping sweat and catching our breath.

Brian squinted, grinning. "So...how was it? You'd been in a bit of a slump, if I recall?"

"Almost a year." I shrugged.

"How long did you last?"

"Four. Five, tops."

"Minutes?"

"Pumps."

He chuckled. "Well, that's the most expensive fuck of your life."

He wasn't wrong. The receipts spoke for themselves:

$500 — Amber's bed replacement
$2,000 — Flights, Ubers, a cabana, bottle service, and dinners in Miami
$100 — Ticket to the White Party in Prospect Park
$400 — Sink replacement

Sex always sends a bill.

I still wonder if she's out there—
gripping porcelain, leaving a trail of cracked sinks and broken hearts.

No goodbye. No trace. Just proof that chaos breathes.

The same chaos that saved the summer.

Acknowledgments

Thank you to my ex-girlfriend.
Which one? All of them.

And to my mom, who somehow put up with all of it.

Photo: Martin Abraham

The Author

Joseph Adam Lee is a Franco-American writer from Lewiston, Maine. He writes with an outlaw sensibility, moving between truth and performance. His work is serious without taking itself too seriously, often finding humor where it probably shouldn't.

He lives in New York City.

Contact Information

Email: joe@therebelwithin.com
Website: www.josephadamlee.com
Instagram: @joseph.adam.lee

Letters & Packages

Red Fox Runs Press
C/O Joseph Adam Lee
909 3rd Avenue
#127
New York, New York 10150

www.ingramcontent.com/pod-product-compliance
Lightning Source LLC
LaVergne TN
LVHW091141080826
845145LV00008B/2220